STALKED
BY BLOOD-THIRSTY SIOUX...

Slocum saw him crawling silently toward them as the moon came from behind a cloud. He saw only the feathers, at first, thicker than the grasses.

Then, the glint of his rifle in the now clear moonlight.

Slocum fired once, missed.

The brave leaped to his feet, charged. Slocum fired his last shot, struck the Indian in the forearm. The rifle clattered as it struck the ground. The Indian drew his knife...

OTHER BOOKS BY JAKE LOGAN

JAKE LOGAN

SLOCUM AND THE BOZEMAN TRAIL

BERKLEY BOOKS, NEW YORK

SLOCUM AND THE BOZEMAN TRAIL

A Berkley Book / published by arrangement with
the author

PRINTING HISTORY
Berkley edition / March 1986

ISBN: 0-425-08664-X

A BERKLEY BOOK® TM 757,375
Berkley Books are published by The Berkley Publishing Group,
200 Madison Avenue, New York, N.Y. 10016.
The name "BERKLEY" and the stylized "B" with design are trademarks
belonging to Berkley Publishing Corporation.

PRINTED IN THE UNITED STATES OF AMERICA

1

Less than twelve hours later the killing would start.

But for now, the camp was quiet.

Dinner had consisted of venison, beans, and biscuits of surprising lightness considering that they had been made in a chuck wagon that looked only slightly cleaner than a prison outhouse.

Finished with their meal, done with the bawdy and self-serving stories they had told around the campfire, the men now rested their weary bodies in bedrolls reeking with the musk of body sweat. Pushing five hundred independent-minded longhorns was not easy. Tomorrow they were to pick up the Bozeman Trail and finish the drive to Virginia City, the mining town that had gotten suddenly rich, where beef sold at a premium.

Away from the others slept a tall man whose hair in the dying campfire light was the color of anthracite coal. Even in repose, even in attire as simple as a rough-hewn gray cotton shirt and jeans, there was a special quality to his angular face, an intensity that was part melancholy, part wariness. The War, a part of which he had spent riding with a bloody legend named Quantrill, and which had seen the death of his parents and his brother, had left John Slocum scarred. He rarely slept easy.

In the distance a wolf howled.

John Slocum's face twitched. Even asleep, he was attuned to possible danger. That was why, five minutes later, he came full awake, his .31 Colt Navy filling his hand.

The man might have been a phantom from a nightmare. Slocum's War-years nightmare.

Dressed in the blue of a Union uniform, the sergeant stood in the light from the fire, a .44 Army Colt held at his side, not pointed directly at Slocum. His paunch dripped over his wide strap of a belt and muttonchop sideburns framed mean, pinched eyes.

"Who the hell are you?" Slocum snapped, still groggy from sleep. "And you better have a damned good reason for rousting a man from a sleep he by God needs more than the sight of an ugly face."

"Sergeant Davies. I've got a message from Colonel Carrington."

At the name Carrington, a brooding shadow flickered across Slocum's face.

Colonel Henry Beebee Carrington was known for two things: his temper and his incompetence. During the War he had not spent a single minute in battle. Rather, he had trained troops who would later go to their bloody deaths with his instructions still filling their ears.

After the War, Carrington came west, where he was instructed to keep things both safe and peaceful here in Indian country. But he was not given to a clear head, so many of his plans had gone awry. He made up for his bad record by being demanding and overly harsh in his treatment of both Indians and certain whites alike. He had no time for refugees from the South.

Now he had come into Slocum's life. And Slocum wasn't sure he much cared for the feeling.

Sergeant Davies said, "I believe you're holding a gun on me."

Slocum dropped his eyes to his Colt and shrugged. "Seems I am," he said, but he made no move to drop his weapon.

Something was very wrong here.

"What happened to Bryant, the man on guard?" Slocum asked.

An unpleasant smile crossed Davies's face. "I hope you're not paying him much more than a few dollars for this whole drive. He surely ain't worth it."

Slocum uncoiled his long, lean body and got to his feet. Anger shone in the panther-green eyes. "I don't believe you answered my question about Bryant."

Bryant was a sixteen-year-old whose parents Slocum had known, in Georgia, back before the War. Slocum felt personally responsible for the lad's well-being.

The unpleasant smile came to Davies's face again. "He'll have a bump on the back of his head but otherwise he'll be all right."

"You hit him?"

"Seems I did."

"Maybe you'd better explain why."

Davies shrugged. "I planned to step up and introduce myself but then I saw that this kid didn't hear me at all. And I was right behind him. Figured I'd test him out a little. See how close I could come to clubbing him before he'd hear me. The kid must be deaf. I knocked him out without him even turning around once."

Slocum worked his jaw muscles. The kid was green,

no doubt about that, but Slocum didn't need the help of a swaggering Union sergeant to bring the kid along.

"Where is he?" Slocum said.

"Right where I left him, I reckon."

Slocum brushed past the sergeant and went into the bird-filled dawn. The coral sky and the greening land were alive with robins and jays and crows.

Several hundred yards away Slocum could see the longhorns sprawling over the countryside, feeding early.

Bryant had been walking east to west with a Remington, standing guard against any Sioux with rustling ideas.

He found the boy at the base of a gnarled oak.

He shoved the pistol in his belt and knelt beside the youth. The kid was starting to come around.

Freckled, pug-nosed, and lanky, Tommy Bryant favored his mother. Before starting the drive, the kid had borrowed two gold pieces from his father so he could buy the kind of clothes he thought cowboys wore. He had gotten his information about cowboy culture from reading Ned Buntline stories. His clothes said city dude, and were a source of gentle kidding from the hardcases Slocum, as trail boss, had hired for the drive.

"You all right, Tommy?"

Bryant looked up with the innocence and fear of a newborn. "I don't know what happened," he said softly, a note of bewilderment in his voice.

Slocum helped him to his feet. He walked him around for maybe ten minutes, making sure the kid didn't show any signs of concussion.

Tommy Bryant seemed to be all right. Slocum brought the kid back to camp and had Jonah, the cook, tend to him.

The camp came to life then, the silence of dawn broken by the low din of men cursing good-naturedly and the stamp of snorting horses.

"Another back-breaking day," said one man.

"You ought to ride drag so's you can skip breakfast grub," cracked another. "That dust ain't half bad once't you get used to it."

Several of the drovers stood in a small group looking at Sergeant Davies as if the man had brought leprosy into the camp with him.

Slocum stalked up to the soldier and said, "Good thing the kid's not hurt serious."

Even though Sergeant Davies was no West Pointer, he was intelligent enough to see that Slocum was not a man to push.

Slocum fought down the anger. It was building in him, plain for all to see.

Sergeant Davies backed off and looked away from Slocum's hard eyes.

The moment passed.

"Get that grub out, Cookie," he gruffed. "We ain't got all day."

Jonah Ayers was already frying bread and getting the honey ready to pour on it. The aroma twisted Slocum's gut in a vise of hunger.

Slocum was impatient to eat and get going. Today was the day they pushed onto the Bozeman Trail, the fort-lined passageway that led from Julesburg, Colorado and stretched to Virginia City. The forts protected drovers and pilgrims alike from the quirky habits of Red Cloud, the Sioux chief who was viewed by many as one of the white man's most implacable enemies.

Slocum was anxious to be done with the drive for at least two reasons. One, the grind of a cattle drive demanded rest and relaxation eventually. Two, memories of the War were crowding him especially hard these days. With the two thousand dollars cash he would get for delivering the cattle, he planned to go to San Francisco and spend time eating good grub, taking in some good entertainment and, not least of all, squiring the good women—and in Slocum's book they were all good.

The honcho looked at Davies, caught his eye once more.

"You haven't told me why you're here," Slocum said.

Sergeant Davies smirked. "Haven't had much of a chance, what with you fussing over the youngster."

Slocum bristled. "His folks are good friends of mine." His eyes narrowed. "They fought hard in the War."

Sergeant Davies nodded. "I guess I don't have to ask on which side."

"No, I guess you don't. Now, why are you here?"

Sergeant Davies took a crooked cheroot from inside his blue jacket and stuck it in his mouth. "You met up with a post rider yesterday."

Slocum thought back over the past twenty-four hours. He had indeed met such a man.

"So?" Slocum said.

"You discussed your plans with him."

"We talked, yes."

"Well, he spent the night at Fort Reno. He happened to mention you to me and what you planned to do."

"Which is?"

"Which is to use the Bozeman Trail for your herd."

"Last I knew of, that's why the Trail came into use. To protect drovers. Among other people."

Sergeant Davies shook his head and consulted his cheroot as if it were a crystal ball. "Afraid you can't use it these days."

Slocum's stomach knotted up. There was the anger again, boiling inside him. For a number of reasons, the Bozeman Trail was absolutely the best route to Virginia City, the fastest and the safest.

If he couldn't use the Trail, his delivery date would be missed, and there was a very good chance that, between Indians and rough country, not everybody, nor every head of cattle, would make it. There was no way he was going to be denied using the Bozeman Trail.

"I'm going to use it," Slocum said.

Sergeant Davies shook his head again. "Colonel Carrington issued an order a couple weeks ago."

"Afraid I'm not impressed."

"You know who Colonel Carrington is?"

"I know who he is."

"Only one who can rescind the order is the colonel himself."

"Where do I find him?"

"Fort Phil Kearny."

"In other words, I have to get to Virginia City before I get his permission?"

"Afraid so," Davies said.

"That doesn't make any sense."

"The colonel's only thinking of everybody's well-being."

"You mind if I don't get all choked up? I been looking after my own well-being for quite a spell," Slocum said.

Davies sighed. "Don't matter if you believe him or not, but what with the Indian troubles lately, the colonel just don't feel it's safe for drovers and pilgrims to be on the Trail. The army wants him to guarantee the safety of people and, given present conditions, he can't."

"Who's in charge at Fort Reno?"

"Captain William F. Scott."

"I'll talk to him."

"Won't do no good."

"I guess I'll just have to take that chance, won't I?" Slocum said.

"The captain," Davies said, "does everything the colonel tells him."

"I'll bet he does," Slocum said sardonically. Slocum waved in the direction from which Davies had come. "Probably be a good time for you to be on your way, soldier."

"I sure wouldn't want to make Colonel Carrington mad."

"Right now, with five hundred head of longhorns needing delivering to Virginia City, I can't say I'm unduly mindful of what the colonel wants one way or the other.

"He's got a bad temper."

"You're stretching mine pretty thin, Davies."

For a long moment the two men stared at each other. Davies looked as if he might vaguely be considering drawing his weapon again. He looked long and hard at the butt of the pistol jutting out of Slocum's waistband. The banter among the men around the chuck wagon died down and faded away.

A horse snorted. A tin cup slid across a tin plate with a soft scraping sound.

"Tell your Captain William F. Scott that I'm coming to see him this morning," Slocum said.

Davies shrugged and moved away. He caught up his horse and rode away from the camp. A couple of drovers laughed. The tension broke like a string stretched too tight for too long.

Jonah brought Slocum's breakfast over. "Sounds like we got ourselves some trouble, John."

"Maybe," Slocum said, looking down at the plate. Something sour stirred in his stomach.

2

Three hours later, the late summer sun hot on his back, Slocum rode up to Fort Reno. The gates were open. He rode to a hitchrail outside and dismounted. He started to walk through the gates when a strange sight caught his attention.

A stout woman in a prim black dress that covered every bit of her body save for her oddly handsome face stood swinging a heavy satchel at a thin man whose low-slung Navy Colt marked him as a gunfighter.

The situation would have been comical—the woman angry and devastating with her satchel, the gunfighter cackling like a drunken sourdough as he moved in and out of the satchel's range—except for one thing.

There was a full-grown man hiding from the gunfighter behind the stout woman. Literally behind her apron strings, because over her girth was wrapped a piece of cloth as black as her dress.

Slocum wondered what kind of man would let a woman defend him.

Deciding it was none of his business, Slocum started

to make his way toward the small cut-timber wall that was Fort Reno, its handful of buildings hidden behind the timber.

The doings outside the fort reminded Slocum of a traveling circus encampment he had once seen.

Wagons of virtually every description stood in a wide semicircle on the grassy plain. From what he could glimpse of their cargo, Slocum reasoned that the wagons were loaded with dry goods and retail goods, presumably to stock some kind of mercantile store. Farther west, in places like Virginia City, gold-rich men and women wanted the finer things from back East.

Beyond the wagons a few dozen horses and pack animals milled inside a rope corral, a small herd obviously going up the Bozeman Trail to be sold at some prearranged destination, much as Slocum's longhorns would be sold.

Closer by, a bull-whacker was showing off for some children, cracking his whip with a snap that sounded like a gun being fired. The bull-whacker was cutting wax candles in half. He was a thickish man who wore a faded Union army shirt that a few years ago, probably in the War, had been part of his uniform. He seemed to want to hang on to the memories. A lot of men wanted to, apparently, but whether out of pride or bitterness, Slocum had no idea.

Near a campfire that was being readied for lunch, two black people of middle age worked over a raw piece of beef that would go into the boiling pot for stew meat. The black man nodded to Slocum as he passed. Slocum returned the courtesy. The man had been the first person here to pay Slocum any attention, let alone be polite to him.

Because he had been greeting the man, Slocum didn't

see the pair of long legs sticking out in front of his path.

He tripped, grabbing the wheel of a Conestoga wagon for balance.

"Hey, sumbitch," said an irritated male voice. The fleshy man with the balding head and the hound-dog face was obviously peeved that Slocum had tripped across his legs.

The man had been propped against the wagon, his legs out in front of him, resting in the shade.

Slocum had to wonder what an able-bodied man was doing asleep at this time of day.

Before he had a chance to wonder any more, a melodious female voice from the front of the wagon said, "Lee, are you bothering people again?" There was tolerance and amusement in the voice.

Then she poked her face around the edge of the wagon. John Slocum rocked back on his heels.

She had red hair piled atop her head, exposing a surprisingly open, classically endowed face. Her hair was as fancy and pretty as any he had ever seen. The woman would have looked right at home at the San Francisco Opera House.

Her nut-brown eyes shone with interest and curiosity as Slocum doffed his Stetson and bowed his head slightly in deferential greeting. She made a move to climb down from the wagon. Slocum was quick to offer his assistance.

She was a slight woman in her mid-thirties. Her white, high-necked blouse and modest flared skirt could not hide her full-bodied beauty. Melon-sized breasts pushed at the fabric of her blouse. Slocum felt his mouth go dry.

"I'm Emily Schoolcraft," the lady said, putting out a delicate hand. Slocum took it, felt the warmth of her touch.

As they made their first physical contact, Slocum noticed that the man he'd tripped over had gotten to his feet. The man did not look pleased. He dusted off his flat-crowned hat and glowered at Slocum.

"Why don't you run and find my sisters, Lee?" the woman said. "Tell them it's getting on to lunch time."

Her eyes did not leave Slocum's while she spoke.

Grumbling, the man departed.

Slocum, too long between women thanks to the demands of longhorns, finally let go of her hand. It was something he did not want to do. His palm, still warm from touching her, went slick with sweat.

Emily Schoolcraft made a clucking sound. "I suppose some day we'll have to get rid of him."

Slocum, whose mind was more on the carnal possibilities of Emily Schoolcraft than what she was saying at the moment, tried suddenly to focus his mind on her words. It was no use. He hadn't understood what she'd just said.

As if sensing that Slocum was slightly agog in her presence, Emily Schoolcraft laughed. It was a wonderful, throaty laugh that prickled his senses, made the hackles bristle on the back of his neck. He stared reverently at her breasts, in particular at the suggestion of roseate nipples through the thin fabric of her blouse.

"I was talking about Lee Dimmock," she said, nodding in the direction of where the man had been sleeping.

"Oh. Yeah."

"We met him in Ohio. We had need of a driver and protection, my sisters and I. You see, my husband died in the War, while serving with General Canby at the Sabine Pass." She had gotten flowery and formal on him, like a piano-recital student showing off, but it only enhanced her charm.

She shrugged at old memories. "We had traveled around for several years after my husband's passing, but we didn't really feel the need of protection until lately." She shook her red-gold hair sadly. "You know how the modern world is getting to be."

He nodded sage agreement. Then he asked, "You mentioned traveling around?"

"Yes. With my sisters. We help bring the truth to people who otherwise wouldn't know it."

From her skirt she produced, as if by magic, a thick, buckram-bound copy of what was unmistakably a Bible.

"We have a wagonload of Bibles," she said. "Of course we prefer to see it as a wagonload of Truth. Anyway, even when you're helping to spread the Word, you need protection. And that's where Lee comes in. He drives for us and helps keep us safe."

"You must've been working him pretty hard lately."

"Why's that?"

"Him sleeping at eleven o'clock in the morning. He must be pretty tired out."

She smiled. "I think you've guessed my secret."

"Your secret?"

"Yes, we keep Lee around more out of loyalty than for any other reason. We realized several months ago that he's given to a certain amount of shiftlessness, but . . . well, we're trying to make him see the Truth, and we couldn't do a very good job of that if we fired him, now could we?"

"I reckon not."

Despite all the talk of churchly things, Slocum's gaze remained fixed on her breasts. He was a weak enough man where women were concerned, particularly women who filled out their clothes with such grace and beauty as this one.

"Well," she said, and Slocum could see that for some reason she was concluding the conversation, "I'm afraid I have to get back to my work." She nodded toward the wagon. "I spend an hour in the morning and an hour in the evening on my knees praying."

Slocum didn't know what to say. He knew how to compliment somebody for winning a game of stud or picking out gold in a vein of ore, but what could he say to somebody who prayed a lot? Slocum gave the lady a very serious nod and put his hat back on his head.

"I hope we'll see each other again," Emily Schoolcraft said.

"I certainly do hope we will, ma'am."

"Maybe then I'll have the opportunity to teach you some things."

Slocum could imagine all sorts of things he'd like to learn from Emily Schoolcraft.

He put his hat back on and touched his hand to its brim. It was hard walking away. He did not look back, but he could feel her stare burning into the nape of his neck.

The camp smelled of hot grass and horse manure and the stew that was beginning to bubble on a cookfire. All these wagons meant Colonel Carrington had forbidden all these people to travel the Bozeman Trail. Slocum clenched his jaw muscles. He didn't like people who made arbitrary decisions that affected his life. Slocum wanted to deliver the longhorns and be done with the job. The people were stacked up here like cordwood, a damned logjam of travelers.

As he moved toward the fort, one other thing played at his mind. Sexy as he'd found Emily Schoolcraft, sincere as he assumed she was about her religion, he was still puzzled that she would be so confused about where her husband had died.

She'd said the man had served with General Canby at the Sabine Pass.

From what Slocum knew of Union Civil War history, Canby had never even been to Sabine.

Not even close.

Was the woman simply confused? Or was she lying?

And, if so, *why* would she lie? What could she possibly have to gain?

Slocum sensed she was a far more complicated woman than she wanted anybody to know.

Captain William F. Scott's office filled a small log cabin tucked in the eastern wing of the timber wall surrounding the five cabins that made up Fort Reno.

A guard asked Slocum numerous irritating questions about why he wanted to see the captain before Slocum simply pushed past the guard and went inside. He was promptly greeted by yet another guard.

Before the corporal could speak to deny him access, Slocum strode into the commandant's office. The man at the desk was busy reading a sheaf of documents. He was poured from the Custer mold, a military dandy with long blond hair and a fancy uniform that seemed to belong to a European principality. The officer looked up, frowned, then picked up a .44 Pocket Army revolver and pointed it directly at Slocum's chest.

"You'd better have some damned important business," Captain Scott said. "Or you'll pay the penalty." He was a man in his thirties who spoke in a resonant baritone that bordered on the pompous.

"I'd say my livelihood is pretty important," Slocum said, "at least to me."

Captain Scott looked him over. "You don't much look

like a madman, such as some who've barged into my office of late." Scott lowered the revolver.

"I reckon not," drawled Slocum.

"State your business, man. I'm quite busy, as you can see."

"My name's Slocum. I'm driving longhorns. I need to go over the Bozeman Trail. One of your men, a Sergeant Davies, informs me the trail's closed."

Glancing down at the papers on his desk, obviously eager to get back to them, Captain Scott nodded. "That's quite correct, Mr. Slocum."

"I have a deadline to meet. The only way I can meet it is to use the trail."

"I suppose you've heard of Red Cloud."

"I have."

"At the moment he's not very fond of white people."

"Maybe he has a reason not to be."

Captain Scott scrutinized Slocum intently. "Were you ever in the army, sir?"

"Yes."

"The War?"

"The one between the states."

Captain Scott's eyes held tight on Slocum. "Did you wear the blue or the gray?"

"The gray."

"Somehow that doesn't come as a surprise," the captain said with a smirk.

"I reckon not, Captain."

"I suppose you have papers for the beeves."

Slocum wondered if Scott intended his inquiry as an insult, maybe a comment on the ethics of Southerners.

The man was such a jackass, what with his too-fine hair and too-fine uniform, that Slocum didn't even waste anger on him. The only satisfaction some people got, he knew, was in trying to make others feel inferior.

Slocum took out the papers and handed them over.

Captain Scott made a very elaborate show of checking them carefully. He cleared his throat and tapped his fingers against his desk.

Finally, he pushed the papers back at Slocum, not even giving him the courtesy of handing them over, and said, "They seem to be in order."

He put a powerful amount of weight on "seem," as if the papers might be clever forgeries.

Slocum reconsidered. Maybe this man was worth troubling with.

But no. That would be doing exactly what the man wanted Slocum to do.

Slocum put the papers back in his pocket.

"The trail is closed," Captain Scott said.

"I would like your permission to travel it," Slocum said.

"Apparently you didn't hear me."

"I did hear you. Now I'm asking you to hear me. I will assume responsibility for myself and my drovers. We know that Red Cloud is getting ready to make a move, and we're willing to risk that. But we need to move the livestock on the Bozeman to meet our deadline."

"Then you'll have to find another way to reach Virginia City."

Slocum and Captain Scott stared at each other for a long time.

The captain looked uncomfortable, shifted in his seat.

He looked nervous and foolish suddenly, sitting behind his desk that was the width of a stagecoach, with big, matching colorful American flags tacked symmetrically on the wall behind him, with a picture of his West Point graduating class displayed next to a painting of George Washington.

In his heart, Captain Scott probably imagined himself to be of equal stature with Washington. Slocum had no doubt about that.

Captain Scott fingered the walnut handle of his Pocket Army revolver.

"Colonel Carrington is not a man who tolerates disobedience."

Invoking Carrington's name, Slocum thought, was probably a sign that Captain Scott no longer felt sure of himself.

He had to hide behind Carrington, much as the man had been hiding behind the stout woman when Slocum had arrived at the fort.

"Colonel Carrington doesn't have to know. You're in charge here, aren't you?"

Captain Scott sat up straight in his chair, swelled his chest.

"I do not countermand my superior's orders. Sir, the full force of the United States Army will be used against you if you travel the trail. That I promise you. We do not want to anger Red Cloud at the moment, and anyone being on the trail will anger him."

Slocum was against mistreating the Indians or doing anything to make them unnecessarily angry. But he knew of Red Cloud's erratic ways. Even given the Powder River Treaty, Red Cloud failed to guarantee white people safe passage along the Bozeman Trail. It had been Red Cloud, after all, who helped decimate the forces of Captain Fetterman.

Trying to appease the Sioux warrior—the odd thing

was, Red Cloud wasn't really a chief—was the army's business, not his.

Slocum glanced around the wide room. Maps of the entire Powder River area covered one wall. X marks appeared where forts were located.

On a long, white, narrow strip of paper next to the last map was hand-printed the name "Red Cloud." Underneath it were dates and information about where the warrior had been suspected of striking.

Slocum had no doubt that the Red Cloud threat was serious and immediate. The Sioux might be eager to have some fresh beef if it was free. Red Cloud's braves might be equally eager to kill the white people who owned the herds.

But it seemed to Slocum that the choice was up to him. He didn't want the government telling him where he could or couldn't go. He especially didn't want to hear such dictates from a man like Captain Scott.

"Do we understand each other?" the captain was saying. "The army considers the Sioux to be hostiles. We are at war, sir."

Slocum nodded.

"So what are your plans?" Captian Scott asked.

Slocum tugged his Stetson on tighter. "I guess we'll both find out real soon, won't we?" he said, his tone deceptively amiable.

The big man turned on his heel and strode from the office. Outside, on the porch, he heard Scott yelling for an orderly.

Slocum grinned and stepped onto the parade ground.

Captain Scott was not going to like Slocum's plan at all.

Not at all.

3

The meeting was held in the circle of wagons outside Fort Reno.

Present were all the people who had been waiting to decide what to do next, now that Captain Scott had informed them that the Bozeman Trail was closed.

The stout woman in black, Slocum discovered, was named Nellie Loving. The man she'd been protecting was her husband, Alvin. The two blacks were their former slaves, a married couple named Raymond and Maybelle.

The cowboys who had been fighting with Nellie were Texans. Hank Rossiter was the thin man who'd been giving Nellie Loving an undue amount of grief. He wore the dusty rawhide shirt and jeans of a drover. His low-slung gun marked him as something more, however.

His partner was a tall, swarthy man with dark eyes named Dave Shoop. He also wore his gun in fighting style, though he was careful to introduce himself as a drover.

Emily Schoolcraft had gathered these people together

once Slocum had told her of his plans.

A wind came up as the afternoon rolled toward dusk, flapping the canvas of the wagons, giving the grazing horses and pack animals owned by Rossiter and Shoop a respite from the heat.

Slocum said, "I can't speak for you folks, but I'm going over the Bozeman Trail no matter what Captain Scott says."

There was not much of a reaction to this. The people just waited to hear him out.

"I'll admit," Slocum went on, "that the trip could be dangerous if Red Cloud is riled up. But I think that if we all went together, Red Cloud would think twice before jumping us. With some extra guns, we'd be able to stand off any raiding Indians, be they Sioux, Pawnee, or Cheyenne."

The heavy-set woman in black spoke up. "I suppose you're willing to guarantee our safety, Mr. Slocum?" The sarcasm emphasized her mannish features.

"No, ma'am, not guarantee it. But I think with all of us together—"

"Have you ever heard any of the stories about what Red Cloud does to white women?"

"I've heard them, yes, ma'am."

"And you expect us to travel with you?"

"I don't much see what the alternative is, except to sit here. If the Bozeman Trail's bad, you can imagine what the other routes are like."

Nellie Loving grew tart again. "And just what makes you such an expert?"

Alvin, her husband, a small man in a cheap three-piece suit and a string tie, put up a timid hand to gentle his wife down. She pulled angrily away from him and jabbed a finger in Slocum's direction. "You're willing to risk our lives just to get your cattle there on time, aren't you?"

Slocum shrugged. "I'm going with or without you folks. I just thought you might like to go along."

What with his confrontation with Captain Scott, Slocum was getting tired of human nature, at least as represented by the people in and around Fort Reno.

Rossiter, the angular drover who'd been fighting with Nellie Loving earlier, said, "I'm willing to go, Slocum."

Dave Shoop nodded. "Likewise," he said.

Alvin Loving looked sad. "You know, someday," he said in a careful, well-bred voice, "someday these plains are going to be as safe to travel as the streets of Baltimore."

"Shut up, Alvin," his wife barked. "There's no cause to practice your politicking with the likes of these."

Rossiter's face ignited red. Rage glittered in his blue eyes. "You know something, ma'am? Back home, women don't talk so much. And they don't ride their men into the ground."

Slocum watched curiously as Alvin Loving did something both fascinating and despicable. Instead of stepping around his wife and trying to defend her, he actually shrank behind her, hiding.

Rossiter and his partner Dave Shoop both hooted. Rossiter shook his head. "Kind of makes you wonder which of 'em wears pants, don't it?"

In a single stride, Nellie Loving crossed to Rossiter. She slapped the cowman across the face before he could raise his hand to stop her. The blow resounded with surprising force.

Instinctively, Rossiter started to draw his gun. Before the drover got it from his holster, Slocum responded by dropping his hand to the butt of his Colt.

"Cool down," Slocum said.

The speed of Slocum's move startled everybody.

Emily Schoolcraft said, "Praise the Lord, gentlemen, there's no need for violence."

Oddly, instead of agreeing with her, Nellie Loving shot Emily a murderous look. The Loving woman seemed to disapprove of Emily Schoolcraft just as much as she disapproved of everybody else.

"Put it away," Slocum said to Rossiter, who kept his weapon half-drawn. "We've got a long trip to make with each other. No reason starting out unfriendly."

"No reason at all," said a biting male voice, "as long as we do what Mr. Slocum wants."

Slocum turned to find one of the bull-whackers he'd seen earlier standing at the edge of the circle. The man was fleshy, wearing a greasy denim shirt and stained pants to match. He had thinning blond hair and an almost feminine plumpness to his features. Coiled fat and dangerous as a rattler in his right hand was his whip. Supposedly, bull-whackers did nothing more than drive oxen on with their whips. Supposedly. Slocum had seen men who were just as dangerous with their whips as they were with their guns. Slocum had to wonder if this man was one such expert.

"We've got enough trouble here, Calvin Jenks," Emily Schoolcraft said. "We don't need more from you."

Jenks strode into the circle of people, moving with a pronounced swagger. "I reckon I've got a voice in this," he smiled.

"Reckon you do," Slocum said.

Jenks glared at Slocum. "I say we don't know a damn thing about you."

"I reckon not."

"Once we get past Fort Reno, you and your men could

gang up on us and kill us."

Nellie Loving said, "Not to mention what the Indians would do to us white women."

Rossiter, who had slipped his gun back snug in his holster, frowned at the woman.

One day, Slocum thought, those two were going to have it out.

"In other words," Slocum said to Jenks, "you don't know if you can trust me?"

"That's it," Jenks said.

Slocum turned to look at the rest of the group. "Does he speak for all of you?"

There was no immediate response.

Rossiter and Shoop looked intently at each other, eyebrows slightly arched. Nellie and Alvin Loving stared at the ground. Emily Schoolcraft watched Slocum with a glittering intensity in her eyes, her lips curled in a half-smile. The two slaves, Raymond and Maybelle, sat next to a wheel, chewing on blades of grass and watching intently.

"I'll tell you what," Slocum said. "I plan to hit the Bozeman Trail about midnight tonight. It will take me that long to get my cattle up here. Any of you who want to join me are invited. To the rest of you I say good luck."

"You in the War?" Jenks, the bull-whacker, asked suddenly, incongruously.

Slocum nodded. "Not that it's any of your business," he said.

"Care to tell us who you served with?"

"War's over, far as I know," Slocum said, and turned away from the man. He looked at the other people and repeated, "I'll be back here around midnight. Those of you who want can join me."

"You can bet we won't be joining you, mister," Nellie Loving said.

Slocum was not exactly surprised by her response. He nodded goodbye and strode to his horse.

Emily Schoolcraft called to him just as he was mounting his animal. She came up flushed and breathless. A look shone from her eyes. It might have been admiration, or respect.

"You handled them very well," she said.

"Strange bunch," Slocum said. "They act like they all want to kill each other."

Emily Schoolcraft frowned. "That's exactly what they want, I think."

Slocum tightened the reins in his gloved hands. "They wouldn't be easy to travel with."

Emily Schoolcraft held her breath for a long moment, the effort only emphasizing the grace and abundance of her breasts.

"I'd be very easy to travel with," she said. "Very easy." She smiled suggestively.

"See you around midnight, Mrs. Schoolcraft," Slocum said.

As he left the camp, Slocum again reflected on his impression of the people around Fort Reno. An odd crew, easily capable of violence.

Not even the beautiful and bountiful widow woman was without mystery and a hint of something amiss. He kept remembering how she'd gotten her Civil War facts wrong. It seemed to him that a proper wife would know where her husband had been killed and who he'd served with.

Unless there was something funny going on, and she wasn't a proper wife at all.

•   •   •

Around dusk, Calvin Jenks leaned back against the wheel of one of his wagons and poured raw whiskey down his throat. He might just as well have dumped acid down there, the way it burned. To compensate for the pain, he cracked his bullwhip out in front of him.

Two little boys who'd been playing marbles scurried away. From traveling the past three weeks with Jenks, they knew how the bull-whacker was when he drank. A mean bastard, especially if you were from the wrong side of the Mason–Dixon line.

Silhouetted against the canvas of one of the wagons was Emily Schoolcraft.

Jenks's loins stirred. He could imagine her plump breasts under all that cloth, how soft they would be in his hands.

Whiskey dribbling down his unshaven jaw, he cracked his whip again in a far-reaching arc.

The kerosene lamp that had revealed the widow woman's silhouette went out.

The show was over.

Jenks looked up at the purpling sunset, saw the black birds angling against the rising circle of golden moon. The sweet smell of damp prairie grass rose from the evening earth.

All a man needed at a time like this was a woman. Like the widow woman, Emily Schoolcraft.

Again his loins flared. He was going to take her one of these nights, there was no doubt about that.

He was caught up in his thoughts so completely that he didn't notice Captain Scott come up. The military man stood there watching Jenks with a look of total contempt on his handsome features.

When Scott spat, it was obvious he intended it as a comment on the bull-whacker.

Jenks, drunk even earlier than usual tonight, raised his head and stared at Scott as if he didn't recognize the man. A sneer twisted across Jenks's lips. "Well, if'n it isn't Colonel Carrington's favorite little boy."

In a single move, Scott crossed the few feet separating them and kicked Jenks hard in the shin.

Jenks yowled and fell over on his whiskey bottle as if to protect it.

Scott kicked him in the back, the edge of his riding boot catching Jenks at the base of the spine.

This time the noise Jenks made was more like a plea.

Captain Scott's look of contempt never changed.

One thing about the frontier, he thought. It attracted the worst sort of scum. Men and women running from one pig-hole to the other.

Take Jenks here. After service in the War—and he was the kind of man Scott would just as well have seen fight on the side of the South—Jenks got into every kind of trouble imaginable, from arson to horse thievery to murder. But Jenks had one trick. He always knew whom to appeal to. He was a man who naturally gravitated to the criminal element and who listened to that element carefully. For a price—which usually meant his freedom; from a jail, from a rope, it didn't matter—Jenks would tell you what he knew and be gone before the person he had betrayed could catch up with him.

Scott raised his foot and angled it steep and deep into the side of Jenks's head.

This time Jenks made no noise at all. He simply collapsed across the bottle, blood starting to race from his nostrils and his mouth.

Scott smiled to himself. In his first Indian battle he had kicked a young brave to death. He'd never forgotten the feeling.

It was one thing to shoot somebody, or even to stab them, but there was a special kind of power that came from raising your foot and stomping somebody, feeling bones crush.

He reached down and lifted Jenks up. He slammed him hard against the wagon wheel.

The two little boys were back, half-terrified, half-fascinated.

Captain Scott drew his long revolver and aimed it in their direction. They disappeared at once.

By now Jenks was reviving.

"Wake up, Jenks. Wake up."

"Wha? Wha?" Jenks whined through his drunkenness and his pain.

"I need you to help me do something," Captain Scott said.

Once again, all Jenks could mutter was, "Wha?"

"The man who was here earlier today. Slocum," Captain Scott said.

Jenks's eyes narrowed in recognition.

"I need you to help me kill him," Captain Scott said.

Many long minutes before Slocum reached the camp where he'd left his drovers and his cattle, he sensed something was wrong.

Bad wrong.

There was the scorched smell of oiled wood on the air, for one thing.

The smell from the kind of fire a wagon makes after it's been burned.

Then there was the coil of white smoke snaking up against the sky.

Signals from one Indian encampment to another? Maybe. It looked to be so.

Tensing, angry already, Slocum had a good hunch what the Indians were telling each other. His stomach tightened up. He dug spurs into his horse's flanks.

The animal loped under him in long, graceful motions of bunching muscle and damp, flaring nostrils.

It was only a few more minutes before Slocum crested a ridge and saw what the smoke signals meant.

Slocum ground-tied his horse and walked through the camp.

Suddenly, he felt that rush of rage the War had taught him. Three drovers lay in a pile under an oak. They had been scalped. But only after their brains had been smashed in with a rock or tomahawk. Brains poured from the sides of their heads.

Several feet away, where he'd obviously been hiding under the chuck wagon, lay Tommy Bryant. The youngster whose parents had trusted Slocum to protect him was dead as a stone. The youngster would now never realize any of the beauties of young manhood—the touch of a woman's love, overcoming the fears of boyhood, learning that his own opinion of himself mattered far more than the opinions of others. None of this would he know.

Slocum should have taken the kid with him.

Should have.

The two worst words in the language.

Slocum found the rest of the drovers, including Jonah the cook, scalped and piled up like so much kindling behind a granite boulder.

He spent the next twenty minutes shoveling sandy soil deep enough to give the kid a respectable burial. Finished, he went over and pulled the kid from beneath the wagon. He carried him reverently to the grave, then put him in the ground.

Slocum was not unduly practiced at prayer, but he

asked whatever God there was to be kind to this boy now that he'd crossed over to the other world beyond.

At least the boy was at peace, Slocum thought, peace being something he himself had sought since the war days and his shamed time with the butcher named Quantrill, a man who, Slocum had learned too late, dishonored the Confederacy and its principles. His own peace would come only when he had returned to Calhoun County, Georgia, and to the farm he had shared with his brother and parents before the War. Standing at the graveside, it seemed he could almost smell the sweet Georgia nights.

Then the stench of death filled his nostrils and he opened his eyes, finished his prayer.

"Lord, give this boy a home," he said huskily, and said a silent goodbye to the kid.

Instinctively touching his Colt Navy, Slocum turned back to his waiting horse, thankful for the night shadows that hid the carnage around him.

Since the War, Slocum's life had been a series of small missions, most of which had revolved around staying alive in the harsh lands of the West.

Now Slocum had a new mission.

Before long, there would be some Indians who would pay for what they'd done to the kid.

As he swung up on his horse, Slocum wondered about the three men who were missing.

Drovers.

He didn't like to think that they would have simply run away, but fear did ugly things to otherwise honorable people.

Fear could tear down a lifetime of honor.

Slocum went to check on the herd.

If there was a herd left.

• • •

Slocum came to the basin where the cattle had been when he'd left for Fort Reno. He was surprised to see the longhorns, with some bulls and calves mixed in, still grazing across the sloping land.

The three drovers were there. Shadows in the moonlight, they rode along the edges of the cattle, settling them.

Slocum rode down to talk to the men.

Reeves, the only one of the drovers who had reached his majority, rode up and tipped his hat.

"You see the camp?"

Slocum nodded.

"Fucking redskins," Reeves said.

Slocum could see that the young man was ready to cry.

"We did what we could. Me and the others..." He nodded in the direction of the two other drovers. "We was out rounding up a few strays. The Injuns didn't see us. We just stayed hid in the basin. After they finished, we kept the herd together."

"Good work."

Slocum realized how hollow his words sounded, realized what had been left unsaid between the two men.

Obviously Reeves was not pleased with himself, with what he'd done.

"I should've gone to the camp, helped out the men," Reeves said.

He wanted Slocum to forgive him.

"It's all right," Slocum said. "All that would've happened is you would've gotten yourself and the other two killed."

Reeves looked miserable.

"Anyway," Slocum said, "you did what I needed you to do."

Reeves looked confused. "What's that?"

"You saved the herd."

For just an instant, Reeves's young face brightened. "Yeah, I guess we did."

"Come on," Slocum said. "We got a long night ahead of us."

"Where we going?"

"Driving the herd up to Fort Reno."

Reeves looked amazed. "Tonight?"

"Tonight," Slocum said. "Right now."

4

After the beating Captain Scott had given him, Jenks decided it was probably a good idea to stay sober the rest of the night.

Trying to tolerate the pain Scott's flailing boots had inflicted on him, Jenks hobbled through the temporary camp outside the wall of the fort.

Many of the people were getting ready to join the man named Slocum, who had promised to be back and embark tonight on the Bozeman Trail, Colonel Carrington or no Colonel Carrington.

He heard the people talking about Slocum as if the man was some kind of hero.

The bull-whacker knew only too well who Slocum was, who Slocum had ridden with during the war years—none other than Quantrill himself.

The only travelers still reluctant to go with Slocum were Nellie and Alvin Loving. Actually, Alvin never had any opinions of his own; it was Nellie who refused to join Slocum.

The Lovings disgusted Jenks almost as much as Slocum did.

Jenks carried his hatred around with him. He especially hated those men who had worn the gray and who'd ridden with Quantrill.

Jenks had been a Jayhawker. The murders of women and children, the wholesale burning and destruction of farms, towns, even churches had been, in his mind, completely justifiable.

Nits become lice.

What Slocum had done, of course, was an entirely different matter.

In the moonlight, Jenks hid behind the edge of a wagon loaded with dry goods. The wagon edge offered him a good view of Emily Schoolcraft and her two sisters, Pearl and Jennie, who were sitting on the ground on a blanket near their own wagon.

Light from a kerosene lantern touched their hair, fell on their breasts.

Curiously, the women seemed to have little in common physically. They hardly resembled each other at all. Emily was as regal as a princess with flame-red hair; Pearl was rail-skinny and alley-cat cute, her blond hair flowing around her shoulders; and raven-tressed Jennie giggled all the time and weighed about twenty pounds too much.

Jenks had his suspicions that the women weren't even sisters. But, given their Bible-oriented ways, it was unlikely they would lie.

Or so it seemed to Jenks as he peeked around the edge of the wagon in hopes that one of the women would show him something he wasn't supposed to see.

That had happened one night and Jenks had scarcely been able to believe it. He'd gone plumb blood crazy, seeing Jennie's enormous breasts spilling out of the corset she wore beneath her blouse.

Jenks was settling into his reverie when he heard on the distant night air the sound of cattle hooves rumbling over the earth.

Others heard it, too, because a small din of excited voices drifted through the encampment.

Reluctantly pulling himself away from the ladies, Jenks hefted his Remington.

Several feet away, from behind one of the wagons, stepped Captain Scott.

In the shadows the Union officer resembled a statue, his blond hair shiny in the moonlight.

He nodded. Jenks nodded in return.

He knew what had to be done. He held up the rifle and grinned.

Silently, the captain disappeared.

Jenks himself went into the night then.

He had a job to do. For pay. A job he would personally enjoy.

Killing the man named Slocum.

Reeves and his cohorts weren't the best drovers Slocum had ever seen, but they did their jobs adequately, riding in wide circles through the tumbling silver dust that seemed trapped in the moonlight.

The five hundred head of cattle responded to the pressure of good men on good horseflesh. They milled as the point rider turned them in.

Slocum and the other two drovers got the animals settled down over the next hour, and then Slocum rode on toward Fort Reno. One of the men began singing to soothe the cattle and gentle them down for the night.

A chill was on the land, the sparse grass frosty as pewter in the moonlight. The first snows would come within weeks, maybe sooner. Autumn could play fickle tricks. Slocum needed to deliver the cattle before then.

He huddled deeper inside his lined jacket and stretched the legs of his horse.

Lanterns glowed in the darkness. Slocum took that as a sign that at least a few of the people with wagons had decided to accompany him on the Bozeman Trail. The smart ones. Slocum had already started forming an opinion as to why Colonel Carrington and Captain Scott wanted the wagon people to remain in one place long enough.

Slocum had heard of such tricks before.

Everything from cattle to dry goods had a way of getting sold off for a loss when people got scared.

All an enterprising military official would have to say was that the Indians wouldn't attack if the wagons didn't contain things they wanted, and frightened people might part with many of their belongings.

Slocum drew near the encampment. He thought of Emily Schoolcraft once again. He could almost see the mysterious, playful light in her eyes. He didn't doubt the sincerity of her religious beliefs, but there was something odd about her, even beyond that.

He started to rein his horse down to a walk when the shot cracked the stillness. An orange flame blossomed on a knoll off to his right. He heard the hiss of the bullet frying the air.

Then Slocum was falling from his horse.

Emily Schoolcraft looked up from her Bible when the shot rang through the prairie night.

Across from her sat Pearl and Jennie, open books in

their laps. They were studying a chapter in the Old Testament.

At least Jennie was. Pearl was in one of her moods—silent, distracted, intense.

Emily sighed. The good Lord did things for his own reasons, and the way He'd seen fit to treat Pearl lately ...All Emily could think of was the night in St. Louis when she'd walked in and found Pearl in that room.

The shot cleared her mind of the memory. Instantly she thought of the tall, lanky stranger named Slocum.

He was supposed to return to the camp. Could that shot have been at him?

Jennie and Emily exchanged nervous glances.

Pearl just sat on her cushion in the corner of the wagon, as if nothing at all had happened.

Emily glanced at her again.

In New York once, Emily had passed a school where simple-minded people stayed. She remembered the strange fascination of their eyes, the way they stared. She sometimes wondered if Pearl might not be like them.

"What do you think it was, Emily?" Jennie asked, nodding outside.

"I hope it's not Mr. Slocum."

A slow, sweet smile appeared on Jennie's cheeky face. "You like him, don't you?"

"He's a respectable man," Emily said. That was the way she judged men out here in what she sometimes called "the wilderness." They were either respectable or despicable. Emily was a long way from the refined parlors of St. Louis where the three ladies had lived for several years.

She touched her Bible and closed her eyes. Her lips moved as she murmured a silent prayer for the well-being of the man named Slocum.

There were voices outside.

"Someone's been shot!"

"Who was it?"

"That stranger!"

"I'm going to see what happened," Emily said tightly.

She had an image of Slocum lying dead in a pine coffin.

She hurried from the wagon.

Jenks, whose shot had knocked Slocum clean from his horse, turned from where he'd been crouched in the knoll's tall grasses to find a surprise waiting for him.

The lazy bastard who traveled with the three School-craft sisters stood there watching him.

Lee Dimmock.

"How long you been here?" Jenks demanded.

A smirk played across Dimmock's face. "Long enough, I'd say."

Jenks lowered his Remington to Dimmock's middle section. "You want the same thing he got?"

"Huh-uh, I want the same thing you got."

"Meanin' what?" Jenks said, his breath pluming ghostly in the chill night.

"You got a kind of sweet deal with Captain Scott, from what I figure. You get rid of Slocum and you two and Colonel Carrington's going to split a nice take from five hundred head of cattle."

"So you want some of it, too?"

"You got that right, friend."

Jenks snorted. "You never worked a day in your life, you lazy bastard."

Instead of being offended by Jenks's words, Dimmock

seemed almost pleased by them.

"Not so's you'd notice," he laughed.

"Well, you're gonna have to start workin' hard now, let me tell you."

"Doin' what?"

"Watchin' your back," Jenks snapped. "Because you never know when I'm gonna sneak up on you and kill you."

The slow smile again touched Dimmock's face. "Maybe I got myself protected."

"How would that be?"

"Lots of people say I'm lazy," Dimmock laughed. "But nobody said I was stupid. Let's just say I got myself protected and if you don't cut me in or you try to kill me, you'll have a lot more trouble than you'll be able to handle, Jenks."

For the first time there was steel in Dimmock's voice and Jenks could see that the man, whatever his short-comings, was anything but an idiot.

"What do you want exactly, Dimmock?"

"Slocum's cattle's going to get sold. I want a fourth of the proceeds."

"A fourth!" Jenks protested.

"Oh, I don't expect you to be reasonable about it. That's why I want to go have a talk with Captain Scott."

"When?"

"Right now."

Jenks kept his rifle on the man. Captain Scott was going to be furious that Jenks had managed to get himself found out.

"I want to go with you," Jenks said.

"I kinda figured you would." Lee Dimmock smiled. "I kinda figured you would."

• • •

Slocum struggled to his feet, clutching his hand to his right hip. The high cantle of his saddle had deflected the bullet enough, soaked up its energy, so that the wound couldn't be too serious. If anything, falling and smacking his head against the ground had hurt more than the grazing bullet.

His hand came away sticky with blood.

Slocum got on his horse and rode the rest of the way to the encampment.

His eyes scanned the long night shadows.

His assailant had obviously been waiting for him, hiding in the tall bluestem grasses on that knoll to Slocum's right. His fall had knocked him cold. By the time Slocum had regained consciousness, the bushwhacker was gone.

He wondered now if he had done the right thing, asking the other people if they wanted to join him on the Bozeman Trail. He sensed treachery in many of their hearts, and trouble ahead because of that treachery.

Emily Schoolcraft ran over the wet silver grass to greet him. "I heard a shot," she said. She sounded as if she were about to burst into tears.

Slocum could see several people: Nellie and Alvin Loving; the servants, Raymond and Maybelle; and the gunfighter drovers Hank Rossiter and Dave Shoop, standing in front of the wagons watching Slocum and Schoolcraft.

"Nothing too bad," Slocum said. "Probably nothing more than a flesh wound that needs a little cleaning."

Pulling her shawl tighter around her, Emily said, "Come to my wagon. I'll clean it for you."

Slocum nodded and dismounted.

The people grouped around him.

Hank Rossiter said, "Seems like you got enemies, my friend." He flashed a half-grin as he said it.

Slocum surveyed the gunfighter carefully. Could Rossiter have been the one who shot at him?

"Most people do," he said, and walked on.

Nellie Loving stepped in front of him. "I demand an explanation," she said.

"For what?" Slocum asked, trying to stay level. He glanced around at the little group of people who might be his traveling companions. Minute by minute, he was thinking less of them.

"For why somebody would shoot at you. Are you the sort of man who attracts violence?" There was a hint of hysteria in her voice.

"Now, honey," Alvin Loving started to say nervously.

"Shut up, Alvin," his wife barked.

The two gunfighters cackled.

"I don't know what you're trying to get at, ma'am," Slocum said.

"Seems funny to me that the rest of us have been traveling nearly three weeks together now and none of us got shot at. But you show up and somebody opens fire. Doesn't that seem funny to you?"

Without hesitating, Slocum said, "Maybe you're the one who fired at me, ma'am."

5

Leaving the stout woman gasping like a landed fish, Slocum followed Emily to her own wagon.

When Emily threw back the canvas flap and helped him inside, Slocum saw something that was right out of a Georgia parlor in the peaceful days before the War. There in the soft lamplight sat two attractive women, knitting and humming gently to themselves.

Slocum felt a number of things at the moment: nostalgia for the way he'd grown up, a weariness that made him want to put his head in one of their laps, and a faint tug at his loins.

"My sisters, Jennie and Pearl," said Emily, taking Slocum's hat and showing him a place to sit. Her sisters scooted out of the way.

Jennie seemed easygoing and simple to understand, a plumpish woman who took great pleasure in being polite and friendly. Slocum noticed immediately that she looked nothing like either of her sisters.

Pearl was another matter. The pretty, graceful blonde only whispered a hello. But it was more than just her quietness, which could have been simple shyness. There was a little-girl quality to her, a disturbing quality, a sense of great and abiding injury in her eyes.

Slocum felt moved by her, but also slightly uneasy around her.

"Are you afraid?" Emily said as she pulled away his trousers and began cleaning out the wound. It was only a furrow through the fleshy part of his thigh. Slocum winced as she poured raw alcohol into the torn flesh.

"Afraid?" he asked.

"Of somebody trying to kill you again."

He shrugged. "Oh, they'll likely try again. If they missed once, that's only going to make them all the more determined."

"But you're still going to take us with you?"

"If you want to go."

"You don't think it was one of us—one of the people in the wagons here—who shot at you?"

"Maybe. Probably."

Emily looked shocked. "Then why would you want us to join you?"

"Selfishness."

Emily shook her head. "You're a mysterious man, Mr. Slocum."

"Captain Scott would likely try to stop me from going on the Bozeman Trail. He's got me pegged as just another saddle tramp. But you people, or some of you anyway, are upstanding citizens. There'd be hell to pay if he did you any harm. So, in a way, you're my ticket. As long as I've got you with me, he's got little choice but to let the bunch of us go."

Emily smiled. "I guess it works both ways, then."

"How's that?"

"There's nobody else who's strong enough to lead us up the trail except you."

Jennie giggled. "We could always get Lee Dimmock."

Emily scowled. "Now, it's not our right to judge, sister dear."

Jennie shrank back at the reprimand.

"There's not a natural leader among the group," Emily said. "That's been our trouble. We've been sitting here for days while Captain Scott made up his mind what to do about us. You're our first real hope. Everybody talked it over tonight, and we've decided to go with you."

"All except the Lovings," Jennie said, glancing meaningfully at Slocum. "Seems Mrs. Loving doesn't have a very high opinion of you."

Slocum smiled at Jennie, but his interest focused on Pearl. She had stopped knitting and just sat there, staring intently at the long, sharp needles, almost as if she were considering plunging them into her eyes.

Emily followed his gaze. "Are you finished knitting, dear?" she asked the younger woman.

Pearl looked up. In the soft glow of the kerosene lamp, sitting in the middle of a multi-colored quilt, she resembled a doll. A beautiful but very troubled doll.

Pearl smiled weakly. The smile gave her an odd look, the look of someone demented. Her straw-blond hair made her face appear even more pale than it was, without any rouge on her cheeks or lips. Her gaze finally rested on Slocum. "He reminds me of somebody."

"Who?" asked Emily softly.

"I'm not sure. But I think I know."

The other two women smiled at each other. Obviously they took an odd kind of pleasure in Pearl's strangeness. It was as if they had a child to raise between them.

"You don't know who he reminds you of?" Emily asked again. "Or you think you do know?"

Pearl shrugged, lost completely in her own thoughts now, and went back to her knitting.

Emily finished her work on Slocum's thigh. Blood began to leak around the wound. She quickly dabbed on salve from a tin, covered the dressing with gauze, then a flap of cotton. She handed him a bandage, averted her eyes.

"Wrap it, but not too tight," she said. "You won't want to cut off your blood.

Slocum noticed that Jennie and Emily did not look as he hoisted his bare leg and wrapped the bandage over the other dressing. Only the strange blond woman looked at him with that odd, off-center stare.

Then Pearl said suddenly, in a high, eerie voice, "He reminds me of the man in St. Louis. The man who—"

"That will be enough, Pearl," Emily said. Her voice was harsh and sharp. Her face suddenly looked older, harder.

Slocum was puzzled. He could hear skeletons rattling in the Schoolcraft closet.

Emily capped the bottle of grain alcohol and dropped the rags she'd used as swabbing into her lap. She took out her sewing and quickly repaired his trouser leg so that the bandage did not show. He watched her deft fingers fly.

"There you are, Mr. Slocum. Good as new."

"John. Thanks. I appreciate it."

Suddenly he felt as if his welcome was over. Some things had been said here that he was not supposed to overhear. He was the eavesdropper, the outcast. He could feel it in the growing silence.

"I'll say good night, ma'am—ladies."

Emily held out his hat. He put it on.

When he looked up at Pearl she had stopped knitting again.

She held the needles pointed toward him like miniature lances. A strange light crept into her eyes. They glittered like those of a snake about to strike.

Pearl made a slight movement and jabbed the needles forward. She blinked her eyes.

Slocum shuddered as he climbed from the wagon. No one but he had seen what Pearl had done. It was a little thing, maybe, but his mind raced with the thought of what those long, sharp needles could do to a man's eyes.

Half an hour later, Hank Rossiter and Dave Shoop came up to Slocum. John had arranged for supper to be sent out to his drovers. His wound nagged him so that he was not hungry. He would pull on some jerky once they got going. He had told his men to make no mention of the Sioux attack. If word of the massacre reached Captain Scott, he'd probably put Slocum in irons.

"We're going with you, Slocum," Rossiter said.

Slocum, who was checking his cinches, turned to the men in the night shadows and said, "Fine with me."

"We'll be running our herd right behind yours," Rossiter said.

"Run 'em on in with mine. We'll cut them out when the time comes. Tell my boys I said it was okay."

"Fair enough. If the captain lets us go." Shoop smiled with sharp teeth that looked bad even in the darkness. He had one dead-looking eye and curly black hair that gave him the look of a pirate. He was bad company by the worst of standards.

In the lantern-shot darkness, men checked harness, moved horses into wagon traces, threw on blankets and saddles. A man tinked at a nail in his horse's shoe, driving it home with a blacksmith's hammer.

Brute oxen were led to the fronts of wagons. Mules were tied behind. Rossiter and Shoop left to run their herd in with Slocum's.

Dust rose up over the camp to cloud the dark sky.

Slocum was about to mount his horse and return to the herd when Raymond, the black man, came up and cleared his throat.

"You take us with you, mister?" Raymond asked.

Slocum guessed the man's age to be somewhere in his early fifties. He was a chunky man with graying hair. Even in shabby sharecropper's clothes he bore himself with a slow dignity. He reminded Slocum of some of his friends in Georgia. Despite what the Yankee press tried to portray as the Southern attitude toward blacks, Slocum had always felt that he could genuinely call several Negroes his true friends.

Slocum nodded toward the wagon where Nellie and Alvin Loving sat behind a closed canvas flap. "What are they going to say?"

"Don't reckon they can say much. They claim not to believe in slavery." Raymond's grin was infectious. "Leastways, that's how I understand the Civil War. Mr. Lincoln and all that."

Slocum grinned back. He liked the man. Raymond had made a good point. While many Yankees claimed to hate slavery, many of them, in effect, kept slaves by taking uneducated blacks up from the South and paying them a pittance, which was more than they could make anyplace else in the brutally indifferent towns of the North. For mere pennies a man like Raymond would find himself totally dependent on the continued generosity of people like the Lovings, people who would become outraged if you mentioned they practiced slavery.

"You ever driven cattle?"

"Reckon I could," Raymond said.

"You ride a horse?"

"Better than passing fair, I been told." Raymond shrugged. "Only trouble is, I guess, what do I do with my wife Maybelle?"

"She can ride with Emily Schoolcraft."

"With a white woman?"

"I don't think that'll be any problem."

"If you say so, sir." Raymond's voice revealed his excitement.

Nellie Loving must be some mean lady to work for, Slocum thought.

"I'll go arrange things," Slocum said. "Then I'll come back and we'll go out to the herd."

When he got back to the Schoolcraft wagon, he saw that Emily and Jennie were outside holding Pearl, who looked as if she'd just finished being sick.

"Her moods," Emily explained. "She carries on so, she gets sick to her stomach."

Jennie helped Pearl back into the wagon.

Once again Slocum felt that Pearl was a deeply troubled young woman. Quickly he described the situation with Raymond and Maybelle.

Emily said, "Of course Maybelle can ride with us. I was hoping there was something we could do for her anyway. Nellie Loving treats her terribly." She touched a hand to her heart. "You know the Lord told us to treat even the least fortunate of His people well or suffer the consequences."

Wryly, Slocum said, "Nellie Loving doesn't seem to

be suffering nearly as much as the people around her."

"You say that, John Slocum, without being able to see inside her heart."

He didn't argue with her, but his respect for her rose a notch or two. "You're some woman, you are, Emily."

"Maybe if you really knew me you'd be disappointed."

"I suppose you could say the same thing for me."

"I doubt that, John."

Suddenly her eyes went wide and Slocum saw lamplight spill over her face from behind him.

He turned to see Captain Scott standing a few feet away. On either side of him were troopers leveling a pair of Sharps rifles at Slocum.

Scott stepped forward. "I am told you're about to leave."

Slocum nodded. "We are."

Scott chose to disregard his sarcasm. "The Bozeman Trail is closed. I assume you're taking an alternate route."

"I'm afraid I am not, Captain."

"If you take the Bozeman, you'll be in violation of military orders."

"We're all civilians here."

Captain Scott stepped forward. From his flapped holster he drew his own pistol and pointed it directly at Slocum.

Slocum turned to Emily and said, "Get everybody set and pull the wagons out."

Emily nodded and disappeared quickly.

Captain Scott said, "I don't know what you're up to, but I can promise you you'll be dealt with severely. If the Indians don't kill you on the Bozeman, U. S. Cavalry troops will drive you off."

"You have no call to point a weapon at me, Captain.

As yet I haven't done anything. As I said, we're civilians under your protection."

"You've just informed me of your intentions, sir."

Slocum smiled sardonically. "Who knows? Maybe I'll come to my senses and do things your way."

A horse snorted and stamped its hooves impatiently. Cattle bawled. The sounds of people breaking camp intruded on the long silence between the two men.

Slocum pointed to Captain Scott's revolver. "I don't take kindly to people who point guns."

Now it was the captain's turn to smile, unpleasantly. "Before the war you Southerners could get away with talking like that. Now nobody pays any attention any more."

"Somebody tried to kill me tonight. I don't suppose you'd know anything about that."

"Is that an accusation?"

"That's up to you."

"I am a member of the United States Army. I would hardly be given to conduct like that."

"Yeah, I noticed General Sherman disapproved of conduct like that, too."

"He was a fine man."

Slocum only smiled.

Captain Scott put his weapon away. Then he said, "You've been warned."

"So I have."

Captain Scott nodded to his men and, after a lingering glare at Slocum, he turned on his heel, his men following him in close order.

Quickly, Slocum mounted up and started away. He was trotting out of the encampment when he noticed that Nellie and Alvin Loving sat on their wagon, at the ready. They were joining the group.

Slocum shook his head. It was a night of endless surprises, from the bitter death of the young Tommy Bryant to the attempt on his own life.

People hid behind lies, Slocum knew. Captain Scott knew more than he was saying about the bushwhacker. Maybe about the Sioux as well.

Slocum was in a land not his own, and not all of the hostiles had red skin.

In his cabin, which he had appointed much like his room at West Point, Captain Scott broke out his best bottle of Scotch whisky.

Stripping off his uniform to his longjohns, he sat on the edge of the bed and smiled. All he could think of was the price Slocum's herd would bring in Virginia City.

Slocum, one more dumb ex-Confederate who considered himself so intelligent, had done exactly what Captain Scott had guessed that he would do.

He had asked to continue on the Bozeman Trail. After a show of reluctance, Captain Scott had been glad to let him do so.

After all, the prairie was a good place to let Jenks have a second chance at killing Slocum. Then they would sell Slocum's herd for a good price in Virginia City and Captain Scott would have a little more to save for his eventual trip back to Washington, where his uncle, a man in the War Department, had promised to find him a good military position in a year or two.

With all the herds Captain Scott and Jenks had commandeered over the past four years, the good captain would return to the glitter of the capital city a very wealthy man.

Slocum, on the other hand, would just wind up a dead man.

6

For the next four hours the caravan of wagons and animals rumbled and plodded along the Bozeman Trail. Slocum called a rest and set out pickets until dawn. The sun came up and, after breakfast, John got the wagon train moving again. They pushed through the autumnal beauty and chill of the daylight hours. Jagged, snow-peaked mountains towered on the horizon, stood etched against the skyline. Buffalo and gamma grasses stood sear-brown in the waning days of fall, hardly enough to sustain the occasional small herd of buffalo that roamed across the trail ahead of the caravan.

The men, except for Alvin Loving, took turns riding point, as watchful for signs of cavalry as for hostile Indians.

Slocum made sure they did not hurry. If they covered eight or ten miles a day, tempers were not likely to flare. He still felt the tension. The beginning of a journey was not the hardest part, he knew.

He had a bad feeling about this group of people, a feeling that no amount of calm, reasonable thinking could help vanquish.

Try as he might, his mind could not leave alone thoughts of the dead Bryant boy, nor of the attempt on his own life.

He tried to lose himself in the raw beauty of the landscape.

It did him no good.

The cattle bawled and billowed up dust. Men shouted at one another, their voices echoing across vacant ridges. A floating hawk circled a stand of white aspen. Wagon wheels creaked, groaning in protest over rough ground. Somewhere a grouse thrummed a hollow log.

He rode on, wary as a cougar.

Alvin Loving put on gloves when his turn came to drive the wagon. A merchant for most of his forty-five years, his hands were too soft to hold the reins without bruising.

If he whimpered, she would laugh at him, as she laughed at so many other things about him.

Loving hied the oxen, the wagon jouncing forward, its cargo of dry goods and pots and pans rattling even above the wooden squeak of the wagon itself.

Nellie slept in the wagon now. Loving was enjoying his time, dreaming of his first wife who had died of consumption when she was only eighteen.

When people looked at Loving they saw a weak man. He weighed no more than one hundred thirty pounds, wore glasses thick as horn buttons, and he struck most people as a pantywaist. What they didn't suspect was that his true passion was the ladies. Though he didn't seem the kind, he spent many hours rushing off into the arms of whores and fallen married women.

Unfortunately, he had done this during his time with his first wife, and even today a kind of Biblical guilt raged through his heart when he thought of how he had betrayed her.

He had no such qualms about Nellie, his present wife.

He had met the woman when he'd still been in despair over his first wife. Nellie had been the mayor's daughter in the small Montana town where Loving had owned a general store. Like many women, Nellie had claimed to be attracted to Alvin Loving because of his voice. He had a booming, beautiful voice that should have belonged to a mountain of a man. It was Loving's most masculine quality and he'd used it many times to seduce women by reading them poetry. He had been particularly successful with this approach among church women, which was why he kept such a hopeful eye on Emily Schoolcraft and her sisters. They made his mouth water.

As the animals trudged on, Loving reminisced about his life since the death of his first wife. He had run the general store until Nellie had gotten the idea that his voice could become his fortune. With his voice as timbrous, sonorous, and persuasive as it was, she reasoned, he should become a politician.

So for eight years they resided around the Cincinnati area where, in addition to working in a large retail store, it was Loving's task to gain some polish. He often claimed to be going to the public library at night to study the masters—everybody from Aristotle to Thomas Jefferson—on politics.

Instead he'd gone to whorehouses, to women who stank beautifully of perfume and tasted wonderfully of the most arcane vices.

In general, Nellie made his life easy. She made all the decisions for him. He had his whores and she had her pupil.

She even fought his battles for him, as when, the other day, Rossiter and Shoop picked an argument with him just to antagonize Nellie. He had learned to live with the embarrassment of having a domineering wife. He no longer even seemed to care.

They would go back to Montana and he would run for the mayor's position that her father used to claim and then one day, if he was as good as Nellie believed, he would run for governor. Things would be much simpler if, as she secretly desired, Nellie could run for office herself. But women on the frontier were hardly taken seriously at all, and certainly not for political office.

As night came again, scattering stars across the arc of velvet-black sky, frosting silver on the buffalo grass, Loving's urges and needs told him that this was going to be the night.

Somehow, Loving vowed, this evening he was going to spend some time with Jennie.

Slocum recognized the sound.

The howl of a wolf. Only this wolf was human.

There was an answering call, and another, until the hackles bristled on the back of Slocum's neck.

The Sioux were out there, then.

Waiting. Watching.

Touching the rifle's butt in its scabbard, Slocum swung his horse easterly, toward a stand of firs at the edge of a small lake. The water had frozen already, and it was only three hours past sundown. Moonlight gleamed silver on the ice.

Slocum, who had been riding point since late this afternoon, turned back to tell the others where this night's camp would be. His breath made smoke on the dry, still air.

The human wolves had gone quiet.

• • •

The herds settled. Emily and her sisters warmed up stew for everybody. Rossiter and Shoop, the gunfighters from Texas, cleaned their guns with oil and rags. Slocum watched them out of the corner of his eye, wondering if they knew the Sioux were out there in the dark.

He had another thing on his mind, too.

When he stripped his horse, laid out his saddle and gear, something white had caught his eye, jutting out of a saddlebag. Someone had walked up to his horse after he'd lit. He read the note quickly, stuffed it in his pocket. He looked around, but saw no one looking back. He drew a breath, walked over to a rock, and sat down wearily.

While others waited in line for their food, Shoop said, "You know, I once heard of a man who hid behind his wife every time you tried to get him to fight."

Slocum looked up.

Alvin Loving, his tin plate in his hand waiting for stew, froze solid as ice in a pond.

Rossiter gave a theatrical chuckle. "Wouldn't hardly call a creature like that a man at all."

"Guess you're right about that," Shoop laughed. "Wouldn't you agree, Alvin?"

"That's a purty name," Rossiter said, "Alvin is."

"Not as purty as the guy what owns it."

Calvin Jenks and Lee Dimmock, who had been sitting over by Emily Schoolcraft's wagon, now got up and moved in a little closer. Maybe they sensed trouble, or maybe they wanted to start some.

Slocum stood up and ambled over too, just in case.

Alvin Loving remained immobile.

Rossiter touched Loving's shoulder. "I said you got a purty name."

"I heard you."

"I wouldn't want nobody sayin' *I* had a purty name."

Alvin Loving said nothing.

Rossiter threw his tin plate in the washbucket and tugged his leather gloves tighter. His eyes glittered ominously.

Slocum watched lazily. Maybe it was none of his business, but he was the trail boss, and Loving was outmatched. He didn't think much of Rossiter for ragging a man who probably couldn't stand up for himself. But he didn't think much of Alvin Loving, either.

Just as Rossiter started to make a move, Nellie Loving stepped down from her wagon. She stormed over to Rossiter, raising her flabby arm.

Slocum grabbed her before she could throw a punch.

"No," he muttered through his teeth.

He took the woman's thick wrist and pulled her away, out of earshot of the others.

"Leave them be," Slocum said.

"He's going to hurt my husband," Nellie Loving snapped.

"If you step in, you'll hurt him worse. That's what this is all about."

"What?"

"You must've stepped in the first time they started to pick on your husband."

"Indeed I did. Those men are riff-raff."

"Your husband would have been much better off if he'd spoken up for himself."

"That Rossiter man, he would've hit him."

"There's a lot worse things in this life than getting punched, Mrs. Loving. Not having your dignity is one of them."

"Are you insinuating that I am taking his dignity away from him?"

"Your husband needs to fight his own battles, Mrs. Loving. That's all I'm saying. And I'm saying it for his sake."

She put hands on hips and glared at him. "The only reason we decided to join you was so we could beat the first snow back to Montana. No other reason at all. Certainly not because I have any respect whatsoever for your judgement."

With that, Nellie Loving stalked away from him.

Slocum followed, back to where Alvin stood watching Rossiter square off against him.

The onlookers had formed a semicircle now to watch Rossiter move in to strike Alvin Loving.

The first blow knocked Loving cleanly off his feet.

Rossiter moved in to kick the man beneath him. Loving surprised everybody, maybe even himself, by rolling away deftly. Rossiter's foot struck a rock.

The gunfighter howled in pain.

Calvin Jenks and Lee Dimmock laughed harshly.

Rossiter moved toward Alvin Loving, who had jumped to his feet. He waded in, swinging wildly. One, two of the punches landed. Loving teetered on his boot heels, but did not go down.

Another wild punch from Rossiter. This one landed on the sideboard of a wagon. This time, when he howled, the sound made everyone wince in empathy. Slocum heard a knuckle crack on the wood.

While the gunfighter was shaking his hand, as if to shake out the pain, Alvin Loving stepped forward, brought his foot straight up, and caught Rossiter square in the groin.

Rossiter hurtled backward, dropped like a stone. Slocum suppressed a smile as the hardcase doubled up in agony, his face purpling with rage and surprise.

Dave Shoop ran up and stood over Rossiter.

"Jesus," he said.

Rossiter groaned, rolled from side to side, his face contorted with pain.

Alvin Loving stood victorious and drew himself up tall. There was a glow to his face that hadn't been there before.

Slocum noticed that Loving had a cut eye from one of Rossiter's wild punches.

But he also had his pride back.

Nellie's eyes met Slocum's.

He smiled at her.

She looked down at the ground quickly, but not before Slocum had caught the expression on her face.

There was pride there, and smugness. But there was something else too.

Fear.

Slocum and Raymond stood in the night shadows of the trees. In the distance, the mountain peaks shone white in the moonlight.

Closer up, in the small hills and the thick stands of pine and fir trees, bristling in slanted rows clear to timberline, an owl hooted.

Slocum was not fooled. Neither was Raymond. He was jittery tonight, and Slocum knew it.

"They's Indians out there, ain't they?" he said matter-of-factly.

"I reckon. You can tell?"

"That hootie owl done sounded like a rooster with the croup."

Slocum laughed harshly. He had thought the same thing. This was not the mating season, and the call had been that kind, throaty, hoarse, deep. The caller was good. He was just out of season.

"My Maybelle," Raymond said, "she won't be sleeping well tonight. Her people were part Indian."

Slocum scratched his head. "I'm going to keep you company tonight. I'll join you in about half an hour. Something back in camp I want to check."

"They's kind of crazy folks, ain't they?" Raymond nodded back to the circled wagons.

"Maybe," Slocum grinned.

"Especially that Nellie Loving. One mean woman, she is."

"Could be she's just scared. Acts mean to cover it up."

"Maybelle told me about the fight. Never thought I'd see the day Alvin Loving would stand up for himself."

"Any horse'll buck if he gets a burr under his blanket. Gentle or not, broke or not," Slocum observed.

This time Raymond grinned.

Slocum drifted back to camp.

The note in his pocket was burning a hole in his leg.

No sense in trying to fool himself. He knew who had written it, and why.

There was just no explaining some women.

Any woman.

She was waiting behind her wagon.

In the moonlight, caped and cowled in crimson, she looked like a city lady out for a winter stroll. Her breath smoked in the icy air.

"A body could get mighty cold out tonight," she said.

"Unless there's somebody to warm it up."

Her huge, beautiful eyes peered out at him from the shadows of the cowl. "I want you to know," she said, "that I have given my heart and soul to the Lord."

Slocum didn't answer. She stood there, her breasts heaving, looking at him with those querulous eyes. It was her move, Slocum thought.

She came into his arms.

The heat of her tongue in his mouth ignited his senses. He felt the fullness of her breasts push against him. His manhood began to swell, pressed hard against the crotch of his Levi's.

"The Lovings have an extra wagon," she whispered.

Indeed they did, a smaller wagon hitched to the big one pulled by their oxen.

"Yeah. I know," he husked.

In the moonlight, Slocum and Emily found the wagon. He helped her up inside and then he climbed into the dark wagonbed after her.

Even in the chill the wagon smelled of spices and flour destined for the shelves of the general store the Lovings planned to establish.

Emily was now more in a hurry than Slocum. As they lay down next to each other, she hitched her skirt up and guided his hand to her hot, waiting sex.

Slocum moaned. With his free hand he reached up and slid his fingers inside her blouse. He touched a bountiful breast with its erect nipple.

Neither of them noticed the cold any more.

She lay back, opened her legs wide and pulled her skirt up.

He pressed against her, felt her fingers working at his gunbelt. She unbuttoned his trousers as he kneaded her nipple, plied her sex-cleft with a single probing finger. She was wet now, eager. Her hand freed his penis, gripped it with shivering urgency.

"I want you to kiss me down there," she whispered.

"And you?"

She shifted her position, dove at his loins. His hand fell away from her breast.

Surprised, Slocum buried his head between her soft white thighs. His tongue sought the spot in her folds.

She reared and bucked like a loco horse but he hung on. When she came, she threw him back against the wagon hard enough that he cracked his head.

"Ow," he whispered.

"Sorry. Oh, what you do to me, John Slocum!"

Emily Schoolcraft was a complicated woman, what with her serious religious beliefs and her carnal lusts that were not much different from those of most women Slocum had known. She was a woman he would doubtless remember when he lay by a campfire on some lonesome prairie evening and thought of days gone by.

Then she was on him.

She pushed him back against two fifty-pound sacks of buckwheat and mounted him by taking his throbbing organ in her right hand and pushing herself down on him hard. Then she rode him, coming two, three more times as he tried to match her pace.

They continued for a dozen minutes this way, his mouth filled first with one breast, then another, his hands filled with the tender mounds of her buttocks as he brought her down again and again against himself.

The pleasure of her made his senses reel. She sobbed as she climaxed again and again as if chain lightning ripped through her flesh, galvanizing her loins. She surged against him until he could no longer stay himself from ejaculation.

He exploded, and the sweet pain made him wince.

She cried out and raked her fingers across his shirtfront. He sank into a sated stupor and lay back, utterly spent.

"Oh, John Slocum," she whispered to him, "you've spoiled me for anybody else."

She slid off him and he took in a breath.

"It was right good," he admitted. "You did all the work."

"Well, next time you're going to do more of it. I promise you."

She played with him, made him want her again.

Skillfully, she kneaded his limp cock until the blood pounded through its veins again.

"I want you," she whispered into his ear. He felt her tongue burrow inside.

This time he spread her legs wide and got on top.

He started pacing himself right from the start so he'd be sure to last longer.

She was wetter and hotter the second time, and his pleasure sweeter, as they thrashed together.

Alvin Loving lay in the next wagon, listening.

This late at night, Slocum and the woman probably didn't think anybody would be awake.

Probably nobody else was.

The sounds they made drove Loving crazy. All he could think of were all the whores he'd bought in his life, all the pretty, perfumed bodies.

He wanted Jennie, wished he were with her.

Tonight he'd tried for a way to make that happen, but no opportunity had presented itself.

Now all he could do was lie here and listen to the sounds Slocum and the woman made, and envy the hell out of Slocum.

When Emily Schoolcraft finished coming the second

or third time—Loving had lost count—Nellie Loving stirred in her sleep.

Loving hoped she wouldn't wake up and spoil his fantasies.

Suddenly he realized how much he hated his wife. How much power he'd given her over every decision. He wanted to go back and run a general store. He didn't want to go back and become a politician and run her father's political interests. He wanted another woman, and long nights of sex such as Slocum enjoyed. He wanted a brand new life without his wife.

He was conjuring up great images of plump thighs and mysterious swatches of pubic hair when he heard the sound.

Someone was climbing into the wagon.

Startled, he half-sat.

A painted and feathered Indian rose above him. A blade in his hand flashed briefly, like a shooting star.

Alvin Loving screamed.

Calvin Jenks and his new partner, Lee Dimmock, who still ostensibly worked for Emily Schoolcraft, stood in the moonlight a hundred yards away from where the wagons had been pulled into a circle for the night.

They were waving the Sioux raiders into the camp, signaling them that everything was clear.

Calvin Jenks smiled to himself. Once in a while things worked out just as you planned them.

Hell, sometimes they worked out even better than you planned them.

Jenks and Dimmock stole away in the darkness, waiting for the Sioux to kill, take white scalps, the same way they'd done it to Slocum's crew a few hours before.

7

In the seconds following Alvin Loving's scream, many thoughts pressed on John Slocum's mind.

He was half-naked and not within easy reach of his weapon. He had been entrusted with the life of the Bryant boy and that boy was dead. Now other lives were in his hands, not to mention five hundred head of cattle that were going to die because the long grasses were at the mercy of approaching winter.

He rolled away from the beautiful, trembling body of Emily Schoolcraft and began pulling on his trousers.

"Who screamed?" she whispered.

"Don't know," Slocum said.

"I'm scared."

"Stay here."

Moments later, Slocum dropped to the ground, pistol in hand. The moonlight cast long shadows among the wagons.

A Sioux wearing buckskins burst from one of the shadows and lunged toward Slocum. His painted face, framed in a yellow headband, showed no emotion.

He flashed a knife, but Slocum saw that he wielded a pistol as well. Army issue.

The Indian closed on Slocum, knife poised, pistol cocked.

Slocum braced himself. The attack was so swift he had not pulled the hammer back, and now there was no time.

Other screams broke out. A woman's.

A pistol boomed close.

Slocum crouched, steady on his feet.

Out toward the foothills where the cattle were bedded down, rifle fire crackled like distant fireworks.

Slocum heard the thump of a heavy-caliber muzzle-loading pistol.

Raymond, then, was in the thick of it.

Slocum spun away from the brave as the Indian slashed with the knife.

The trail boss felt the knife rip through the fabric of his shirt. He doubted his luck would hold for both a bullet wound and a knife wound at one time. One of them was bound to kill him.

The Indian lunged again.

This time Slocum was ready for him.

Slocum brought his knee skillfully up into the brave's groin.

The Indian screeched as he twisted to the ground.

Slocum's knee collided with the other man's head, right near the temple.

Slocum tore the knife from the Indian's hand and plunged it deep into the red man's chest. Slocum felt bone and flesh yield to the ripping steel instrument.

He left the blade in the man and moved to help the others in the wagons.

He saw the Indian crouching in the opening of the

Loving wagon. Saw his arms move, the flash of a knife blade.

Alvin, no longer screaming, held the brave at bay with kicking feet. Nellie was hitting the Indian with a half-full sack of beans.

Slocum shot the Sioux between the shoulder blades. His body sagged. Slocum grabbed his braid, jerked him back out of the wagon. The Indian, dying fast, slumped to a heap at the big man's feet.

The Lovings gibbered at one another hysterically.

Slocum ran now toward a sickening sound, the moan of a terrified woman, the moaning of a woman who was being injured in some way more terrible than mere physical pain.

He knew who the moans belonged to—Pearl—and he knew he must hurry.

Orange flames bloomed in the night as gunfire broke out between those in the wagons and the attacking Sioux.

Slocum kept on going.

He reached Emily Schoolcraft's wagon. Inside, Pearl was screaming now. He stretched out a hand to pull himself inside.

One moment he was reaching into the darkness for purchase and something hard struck him in the head. Lights flashed in his brain. Then he was tumbling backwards into inky and total blackness, his head a thousand throbbing hammers of pain.

Around him the gunfire continued, and the screams and the moans of Pearl.

But there was nothing he could do.

Nothing.

He fell into a chasm swirling with darkness and the sounds turned muffled before they were blotted into oblivion.

• • •

He opened his eyes to see the tear-streaked face of Emily
Schoolcraft framed against a dawn sky.

The light blue background gave him an instant sense
of how long he'd been out.

Despite the pain, despite the disorientation, he forced
himself to sit up and look around. His vision blurred
from the aftermath of concussion. His head felt like a
throbbing stump, lopsided on his neck. He touched a
hand to the lump.

"I cleaned up the blood," said Emily. "You scared me.
I didn't think you were ever going to wake up."

"What happened?"

"We drove them off. But, look . . ." She pointed.

Slocum turned his head. Pain shot through his shoulders, drenched him with oozing sweat.

They had done a damn good job, the Sioux. Three of
the wagons had been burned to charred skeletons. Beneath blankets lay at least a dozen bodies.

Raymond knelt next to one of the corpses, weeping
and rocking back and forth on his heels.

"His wife," said Emily.

On the other side of the camp circle Jenks sat cleaning
his weapon. He was whispering something to Nellie
Loving.

Emily Schoolcraft pressed gently on Slocum's chest,
forcing him to lie back down.

"I was afraid you were going to die," she said. "They
really hit you."

"Yeah."

She shook her head. "They took Pearl. Kidnapped
her."

"Damn," Slocum swore.

He closed his eyes and sank back into unconsciousness.

This time it was chill night when he awoke. He was propped up on bedding inside Emily Schoolcraft's wagon.

A kerosene lamp burned at one end of the wagon, the shadows dancing on the canvas.

Outside the wagon he heard isolated sounds: wolves and coyotes at a distance, the crackle of a campfire close by.

Slocum was depressed. His head still throbbed and all his mind could settle on was loss: the Bryant boy, the people killed in the raid last night, the disappearance of Pearl.

There wasn't a damn thing he could do about any of it. He knew he needed more rest before he could even stand up, let alone track the Sioux.

He went out cold again.

Nellie Loving got up and waddled back to her wagon. Jenks smiled to himself.

During the War he'd seen any number of small towns turn ugly with lynch mobs going after suspected Confederate spies. Jenks had had the pleasure of stirring up such crowds.

Occasionally he would even form them from scratch, find a self-righteous, suspicious, bullying sort who'd be glad to do Jenks's work for him.

Nellie Loving was such a person, and after talking to her for most of the day, he felt sure that she was going to help turn all the others against Slocum.

For the second time, he'd failed to kill the man.

Captain Scott was going to raise hell if Jenks didn't

get the job done soon. But that damned Schoolcraft woman hovered over Slocum like a mother hen.

But, Jenks hoped, Nellie Loving was going to turn things around by repeating the story that Jenks had just told her, by stirring up people the way Jenks had once stirred up lynch mobs.

Then tonight—third time being a charm—Slocum was going to die.

Nellie Loving had never seen her husband act like this. Alvin sat in the rear of their wagon, staring out at the cold night sky.

Usually, when she spoke sternly to him, he responded to her like an obedient dog. But tonight . . .

"I said, Alvin," Nellie Loving commanded, "that I need to talk to you."

No reply.

Alvin Loving sat inside his heavy winter clothes and continued to stare at nothing with vacant eyes.

She crawled through the interior of the wagon. The Conestoga felt as if it were going to capsize.

She put a meaty hand on his shoulder and started to spin him around. As if galvanized by the action, he took her hand and flung it away from his body as if it were covered with germs.

"Alvin," she gasped, her face mirroring her shock.

"Shut up," he said.

He had never said that before. Both of them stood there and stared at each other, having absolutely no idea what to expect of their lives now that one was no longer master, one was no longer slave.

Alvin Loving, without a word, and certainly without asking his wife any sort of permission, jumped down out of the back of the wagon and strode out of her sight.

• • •

Rossiter and Shoop were on night guard with the cattle. They listened as the herd settled down.

Rossiter, watering his gelding, said, "You reckon Jenks knows what he's doing?"

Shoop spat. "Nope."

"Then who's behind him?"

"Don't know yet."

Earlier in the evening Jenks and Dimmock had come up and talked about what would happen if Slocum died from his concussion. Rossiter and Shoop had heard the men out, not quite knowing what to think.

The way Jenks outlined it, the plan was simple enough. If Slocum died, the four men would swear that he'd lost the cattle in a game of five-card stud, and that the cattle belonged, as a result, to Jenks. For going along with the story, and for helping drive the cattle to Virginia City, Jenks would split the payoff evenly among the four of them.

"Virginia City's going to be nice," said Rossiter, shifting his weight in the saddle. He looked over the herd, saw Slocum's drovers on the other side of the bedding ground, out of earshot.

"Yeah," Shoop said.

Then Rossiter said what he really wanted to say. "Jenks is going to help us get richer."

Shoop was curious. "How?"

Rossiter touched his head. "I'm still working it out."

Shoop smiled. "Good thing I trust you, Rossiter. Otherwise I'd shoot you in the fucking back."

"It's been tried, Shoop."

"You get the deck shuffled, I'll look at the deal," Shoop said.

Rossiter said nothing.

Shoop shivered in the sudden chill that crept inside his sheepskin coat.

Alvin Loving found Jennie washing out some of her undergarments in the ice-cold waters of the creek that ran down to the lake. His boot broke a twig as he came up to the woman. She jumped a half foot.

"Oh, Mr. Loving," she said, "you frightened me so."

He tipped his derby. "Sorry for scaring you."

She smiled. "Oh, it's all right. I was just lost in my thoughts." Her face filled with tiredness and grief, the smile vanished. "My sister Pearl..."

She didn't have to fill in the details, what Indians did with white women.

"We're going to get her back, ma'am."

In the vast night his voice had a tinny quality. But there was something stirring in it too.

She couldn't help but smile again. Alvin Loving wasn't the sort of man you expected to hear grand statements from.

The Slocum man, or even the gunfighters Rossiter and Shoop, she could imagine them talking about going to get Pearl. But not Alvin Loving.

Loving saw her expression. "Are you smiling, ma'am?"

"No."

"Please don't lie to me."

"I was just..."

"You don't think I'm capable of it, do you?" Despite the fact that he'd lusted for this woman almost from the first day he'd seen her, there was much more at stake now than simple bodily fulfillment. There was his pride as well. He was tired of being a pantywaist.

"I plan to get her and bring her back for you," Alvin Loving said.

For some reason, she no longer found him a funny little man. There was real determination in his eyes, in the set of his jaw.

"Why, I guess I do believe you, Mr. Loving."

"Please call me Alvin."

"Alvin, then."

And then he did it. What he'd longed to do since first laying eyes on her.

Alvin Loving stepped manfully forward, grabbed Jennie, and swept her into his arms.

His mouth crushed against her lips. To his surprise, she did not resist. Instead, she responded with a savage willingness.

She pressed her full hips into his and took his hand and guided it to her full breast.

Alvin felt her heat flow through him.

He eased his hand down from her breast and pulled her skirt up until he could feel her bare thigh.

His hand crawled down to her sex, fondled her. Her lips massaged his own, wet, velvety. She pulled the other side of her skirt up higher.

Gently he pushed her back against a tree.

His manhood swelled as she worked the buttons of his fly, the blood making it pulse until he grew light-headed.

She worked his penis free, pushing his trousers down past his waist.

Neither said a word, worked at each other in silence.

He cupped his hand around the swell of one of her naked buttocks, his fingers finding the curve of the globe so that when he entered her he had a sense that only a thin membrane separated them from totally being one.

She started to grind and he ground back.

He wanted to come and at the same time he didn't want to come.

He just wanted to enjoy this insane, wonderful moment here along the creek edge with the moon silver in the sky and clouds dragging by like wraiths.

He drove up deeper and deeper until she started to whimper, all the while lapping at her breasts until the nipples were erect and hard as thumbs.

"Oh," she said, "oh, oh, oh."

It was somewhere within all this frenzy and all this realization of his own manhood that he heard from behind him the voice of his wife Nellie.

"As soon as you're done there, Alvin, I'm going to give you both barrels."

Cold, clammy sweat broke out in beads on his forehead as he heard the hard metallic sound that filled him with dread.

The twin click of cocking hammers.

8

"Who are you?" Slocum asked.

Emily Schoolcraft smiled, but there was nervousness in the smile. "Why, don't be silly."

"I'm not being silly."

He had been awake for an hour now, the pain in his head less, his strength seeming to return, thanks to the broth Emily had given him.

He knew he would soon be up and around. In pain, yes, but up and around for sure.

"I don't know what you mean," she said evasively. "My name is Emily Schoolcraft. But you know that already."

"You told me your husband served with General Canby at Sabine Pass."

"Yes. That's true."

"No, it isn't."

She flushed crimson in the lanternlight. "I don't know what you mean."

"General Canby was never anywhere near Sabine."

"Well, I must've confused him with another general, then."

"Seems a wife would know who her husband served with."

She stared at him. "I thought we were friends, John."

"We are." He paused. "Friends are supposed to be honest with each other."

"Meaning what?"

"Meaning you're not being honest with me. Not about your husband anyway."

"I just don't happen to remember the name of the general he served with. It was a very sad time. I don't have much of a memory, anyway."

"Emily."

"What?"

"I want you to tell me the truth."

For the first time she looked at him frankly. "Why?"

"Because otherwise we can't be friends. And right now I really need a friend."

The night was closing in on him. He was leading a small wagon train of people with treachery and deceit in their hearts. Ever since the War the world had been rough to him. He liked Emily Schoolcraft. He wanted their relationship, even though it consisted of little more than enjoyable sex and good will at the moment, to be something he could count on, if only for the next twenty-four hours of his life.

If he lived that long.

"Why don't you tell me about it?" Slocum said gently. "Your life, I mean."

She was staring off into the corner. To a trunk, its lid thrown open, filled with clothes and relics of her days.

In a faraway voice she said, "You wouldn't want to

hear about it, John. Maybe you wouldn't like me so much afterward."

"I doubt that, Emily."

"I am not a good woman."

"Depends on your definition of good. I've never taken that word to mean what most church folk do."

Emily sighed. "All I can think of is Pearl out there. Maybe it would have been better if we'd stayed in St. Louis."

She shook her head, held out her hand, and touched Slocum's hand.

Then she told him.

Emily Schoolcraft had been a nice-looking twelve-year-old when her pa, a religious man who'd farmed rich soil in Illinois, had fallen dead from a heart attack. Emily's mother had died long before. Emily went to St. Louis to live with her Aunt Effie, who, as it turned out, was a madam. At first Emily ran away, not knowing how to deal with a woman as sinful as her aunt. But, after two nights of sleeping in barns and battling rats and stray dogs for scraps of food, she went back to her aunt's and agreed to live under the same roof if her aunt promised to say prayers with her every night.

Over the next few years, Emily, despite her best wishes to the contrary, began learning the ways of the world. Aunt Effie's was a rather exclusive place. The girls had to let Effie examine them every day for any signs of disease. They had to take lessons in culture, which mainly consisted of learning rudimentary English grammar, Effie having just enough bankers, politicians, and other prestigious types to make ungrammatical talk jarring in the perfumed and gilded atmosphere of the huge house.

One night Emily decided to see what a man was like.

She was sitting on the front porch swing when a gentleman in a hansom cab pulled up. He wore a top hat and tails and had clean blond hair. She'd never seen a more refined gentleman. Much as she enjoyed looking at him, she scurried her sixteen-year-old body into the shadows. She went suddenly shy when he looked boldly at her.

But the man was too fast for her. He caught her by the wrist, pulled her into the coach, and flashed a greenback at her.

He poured wine from a fancy bottle his coachman handed him and then he waved the coachman on.

While driving around St. Louis near midnight, she lost her virginity and earned her first money as a prostitute.

She told her Aunt Effie about the experience. The woman waited carefully before forming any opinion. She wanted to see how Emily felt about it. When Emily said she hadn't minded, indeed had rather enjoyed herself, even though she was ashamed to admit it, Aunt Effie took her in her arms and started laughing. Emily soon became Effie's star whore.

That had been ten years ago. The end was far less romantic than the beginning of the story. Effie died penniless in a shabby hospital, of syphilis.

Emily fled the corruption of the city government, which now took more than fifty percent of her earnings, and took her spiritual "sisters," Jennie and Pearl, along with her after an unfortunate incident Pearl had with a leading official.

The man had wanted to beat Pearl, but she was frightened. Some of the other girls didn't mind things like that, but Pearl always declined.

The man started to whip her anyway. There was a letter opener on the bureau, and Pearl picked it up.

When the man got closer, flaying her again and again with his belt, Pearl shoved the blade into his fat belly. She watched his eyes bulge and shoved the knife in again and again.

That was when Emily and Jennie had come into the room.

The authorities wanted Pearl to hang. They did not want any whore to get away with killing a decent man.

And so they had fled, roaming for the past few years until they'd met their lazy worker Lee Dimmock, who had promised to lead them to Virginia City, where they could start their trade again.

As she finished, tears welled in Emily's eyes. In the lamplight she looked soft and beautiful.

Slocum liked her more than ever.

"I'm a whore," she wept.

"There are lots worse things to be," Slocum said.

She sniffed, smiled. "You know the funny thing?"

"What?"

"You know how we pretend to be good women and sell Bibles and preach the Word?"

Slocum nodded.

"The last few months, I've actually started to believe in what I'm saying." Then she shuddered. "But here I am, talking about myself, when I should be thinking of Pearl." She shook her head miserably. "I can't imagine what those savages are putting her through."

She touched Slocum's hand again.

"You know," he said, "I like you a lot more now that you've told me the truth."

The tears came back to her eyes.

"You being serious, John Slocum?"

"I am."

She leaned over and gently kissed him on the forehead. "You'd better sleep a bit now."

He didn't argue. He slept.

Alvin Loving felt his erection shrink inside Jennie. Nellie had appeared out of the shadows and with her came Alvin's old sense of self-hatred and embarrassment.

He imagined that Jennie was laughing at him inside, even though she was probably afraid of what Nellie might do.

"Enjoy yourself," Nellie said to Alvin. "It's going to be the last time. . . ."

Alvin pulled himself out, all desire dead in him. He pulled up his trousers, tucked in his shirt. Then he turned to face Nellie and her shotgun.

"Aren't you the girl who told me how wonderful the Bible was this afternoon?" Nellie demanded of Jennie.

Jennie could only nod sheepishly. Apparently she couldn't find her voice.

Nellie sneered. "Where's your Bible now, you young hussy?"

Alvin opened his mouth. Nellie glared at him.

The three of them stood in the moonlight, their breath pluming out from them, staring at each other.

Finally Alvin said, "If you're gong to shoot, just get it over with. I'm tired of waiting on you."

Jennie started to protest, obviously not wanting to give Nellie Loving any encouragement, but said nothing.

Alvin Loving saw, even in the shadows, the unmistakable impression of hurt on his wife's face. He'd never seen that before—only hatred, bossiness, or plain human cussedness.

She had never been much of a woman, and he was no man at all.

At the moment he felt only contempt and disgust for

himself. He almost hoped she would empty the shotgun
in him. Death could be no crueler than what he was
feeling right now.

Nellie let the shotgun slip from her fingers and she
let out a whimper. She put her hands to the front of her
matronly black dress and ripped. The bodice burst open
and her huge breasts tumbled into view, like frosted mel-
ons in the moonlight.

Jennie, horrified, slipped away into the shadows, leaving the two married people alone.

"You going to suckle my breasts the way you did
hers?" Nellie said.

"No," he choked.

"Bastard," she hissed, pulling her torn bodice back
over her breasts.

He turned quickly away and ran back to the wagon.

Jenks had killed only three men in his life, all of them
Confederate soldiers, and all of them unarmed at the time
of their deaths.

Even so, he had needed the edge of alcohol to do his
duty. Now, half an hour before he was to kill Slocum,
he was getting that edge with the help of corn liquor Lee
Dimmock had so generously provided.

Dimmock, who implied that he had slept with all three
Schoolcraft women as he traveled across country with
them as their driver and handyman, was feeling the alcohol, too.

"Them Rebs," he said, leaning back against the rock
where they sat, "they never had them a general who could
do much more'n polish his boots."

Jenks snorted in approval.

He liked being drunk and in the company of men who
hated the Confederacy as much as he did.

There was a poisonous thrill to it all. You worked your hatred higher and higher, and then once in a rare while—as tonight—you got to do something about it.

He was going to kill Slocum.

Then he was going to get the two gunfighters Rossiter and Shoop to help him get the cattle to Virginia City.

And then he was going to take care of Rossiter and Shoop, just the way he would take care of Slocum.

The starry night, the chill air, left Jenks as he closed his eyes and let the alcohol take full effect.

He thought of his boyhood in Ohio and the hard-scrabble farm he'd grown up on and the way his pa had always beaten his ma until all the kids jumped on Pa and stopped him from killing her. Pa was dead now and, remembering that, Jenks wondered if what the parsons always said was actually true, that there was another, better life past this one. Jenks hoped so, because this one wasn't worth much.

"Hey," Dimmock said, "don't go fallin' to sleep." He laughed and shoved Jenks awake. "You got a long night ahead of you."

Jenks laughed too. "Damned if I don't," he said.

The edge was there now. He just hoped he could keep it long enough to kill Slocum.

9

Rossiter tossed his quirly into the night, its burning edge exploding like fireworks in the gloom.

He tugged his hat lower on his head and started back toward camp.

He had just seen Emily Schoolcraft leave her wagon to join her sister Jennie, who was standing among the aspens, sobbing.

Rossiter didn't know what had happened to make Jennie bawl like that and he didn't give a damn. Women were always crying at the least little thing, and there was something strange about all three of the sisters.

The important thing was that Slocum was now alone, without that damned nursemaid, Emily.

He crept up to the Schoolcraft wagon, flattened himself against the bed, and listened hard.

Inside, he heard the sounds of Slocum's snoring.

The Reb had taken quite a blow from the Indian. Rossiter could not recall seeing a cut that deep or wide without the man dying.

Somehow Slocum had survived.

He eased up to the canvas flap, parted it, then hoisted himself inside.

He found what he was looking for. Slocum did not stir.

He rejoined Shoop well before the two sisters returned to the wagon.

"Looks like we might get Slocum's herd," he said.

"How so?" asked Shoop.

"You'll see." Rossiter was all teeth in the dark.

Nellie Loving raised her head up and wondered where her husband had gone. She had not seen him since discovering him with Jennie.

Maybe he'd left her for good, moved his things into the Schoolcraft wagon.

After finding him with the woman, she was not sure of anything any more, certainly not Alvin.

She lay her eagle-beaked head back on the blankets and tried to fall asleep.

It was hopeless.

She could not rid her mind of the image of Alvin betraying her like that, doing what he did to her.

But she knew what she was now. Self-pity flooded her thoughts.

She was an ugly woman, a manly woman.

She should not have made herself even more despicable by exposing her breasts the way she had.

Years of pain crowded her mind. A joke: "Her old man got the son he always wanted. Just look at her." A nickname, "Piggy," when she was an adolescent. Even a mother who was insensitive. When Nellie was eight years old she'd asked for a blue hair ribbon and her mother had said, "Why, that surprises me, child, I just never thought you'd be interested in such things."

In her heart, Nellie did not blame Alvin for going with the other woman. Who could blame a man for wanting someone more feminine than she?

No, all Nellie could hope for now was to return home to where her father had lived and start all over again, alone.

Surely Alvin wouldn't ask to join her. Not after what had happened.

Suddenly a cold rage came over her. None of this would have happened, she told herself, if that Slocum man hadn't made love to Emily Schoolcraft in the Lovings' extra wagon last night.

The animal noises had awakened both Alvin and Nellie.

And awakened Alvin in another respect, too—awakened him to his carnal desires.

Nellie Loving thought of what Jenks had told her.

That he knew that Slocum was a man wanted back in Ohio for the rape and murder of a schoolteacher.

Now, lying there, her marriage in ruins, having to face the fact of her own ugliness, she began to see Slocum as possibly the worst man she'd ever made acquaintance with.

A rapist—

A killer—

Exhausted from her anger and her despair, she fell asleep, vowing to herself that she would someday repay Slocum for all the grief he'd brought her.

The last of the night stars were fading in the pale cream dawn sky when Jenks roused from a liquory sleep and rubbed a hand across three days' stubble.

He had a curious sense of the day in front of him, as if something extremely important was going to happen and no matter what he did, he couldn't stop it from happening.

Fate, as he'd heard a traveling actor in a saloon refer to it once.

He rolled up his blankets. For some reason he thought of his father. He hadn't thought of the man much for years.

Strange that this morning . . .

Lee Dimmock, his own bedroll snug under a sheltering cedar, stirred now a well.

All Jenks had to do was nod at him.

Dimmock knew what was at hand. They had planned it well into the night.

Jenks was going over to the Schoolcraft wagon and shoot Slocum dead.

Dimmock was going to be his witness that Jenks fired only in self-defense.

Then, finally, Jenks could report to Captain Scott that the cattle was theirs. As for reasons why a man like Slocum wouldn't be missed, Nellie Loving could give them some. She would repeat what he had told her like it was gospel.

Hell, nobody would miss the bastard.

One less Reb. He nodded to Dimmock. Dimmock nodded back.

Jenks hitched his pants higher, checked his Colt, and walked into the center of the circled wagons.

He had to move quickly, before other people came awake, so that there would be no witnesses other than Dimmock.

He stopped and looked around. For a moment, he thought he had heard his father calling him. Calling his name. Jenks shivered in the morning chill.

What was going on?

What did it mean?

Still hot and disoriented from last night's alcohol, Jenks started toward the Schoolcraft wagon. He looked around.

Where in hell was Dimmock?

Lee Dimmock was just starting to pull his body from his bedroll when he felt the unmistakable snout of a six-shooter prodding the back of his head.

Then somebody brought the barrel of the gun down clean and hard on the back of his skull.

Dimmock gasped as a shadow moved just beyond his vision. Then the shadows closed in on him and he sank like a stone into deep, dark pools of mindlessness.

Rossiter stalked away from Dimmock's still form, slid between wagons to cross the open space to the School-craft wagon where Jenks was standing.

With the Colt he'd stolen from Slocum a few hours earlier, Rossiter sighted along Jenks's back and then opened fire.

The pistol roared, shattering the silent dawn.

Now there was only one thing left to do.

Rossiter raced across the distance separating him from the wagon, climbed over Jenks's dying hulk, then dropped Slocum's Colt back into the Schoolcraft wagon.

Rossiter dashed away, streaking between wagons until he was well away. Shoop, his alibi, was waiting for him, talking to the cattle to keep them quiet.

There was a brilliant white light, brighter than the dawn, and somewhere in it a grizzled man with a straying left eye and a smile on his otherwise bitter mouth held out a hand to Jenks.

Now Jenks, in his dying moments, knew why he'd

been thinking so much about his pa.

Because his pa was there. He had been there all the time, waiting for him.

Jenks closed his eyes, and something terrible rattled in his throat.

The camp came awake suddenly.

Nellie Loving, in her waking moments, saw that her husband Alvin was back, sitting like a zombie in the rear of the wagon.

Emily Schoolcraft and Jennie awakened as if somebody had shaken them, hearing the gunfire reverberate in the stillness.

Raymond, the black man, lost in grieving dreams of his wife who'd died when the Indians had come last night, grabbed for his revolver. He still reacted instinctively to trouble as if he were being chased by slavers.

Then Rossiter and Shoop appeared, pretending to be confounded about the gunfire and worried as all hell about the welfare of the people in the wagons.

Slocum looked out at Jenks's body, the pool of blood forming in the dust. He picked up his pistol and sniffed the barrel. The stale stench of burnt black powder assailed his nostrils.

He looked at the two women, saw the accusation in their eyes.

By eleven o'clock that morning the farce was being played out in earnest.

Two sides had been taken on the issue of whether John Slocum did or did not backshoot Jenks.

"He sure had plenty of reason," Nellie Loving said.

She might have been addressing a jury.

All the other people sat on nail kegs or on slatted

wooden boxes as each speaker took his or her turn to shape the verdict.

"Just last night, Jenks told me that he recognized Slocum from a Wanted poster." She then told of Jenks's story that Slocum was wanted for the rape and murder of a schoolteacher in Ohio. Her self-righteous tone was fed by her image of Alvin making love to Jennie. Slocum was to blame, she declared, one way or the other, for all of their troubles.

Slocum, still woozy from his wound and morose, sat under the guns of Rossiter and Shoop, lashed to the wheel of the Schoolcraft wagon.

Yet sleeping for most of the past twenty-four hours had revived him remarkably, given the depth and seriousness of the wound.

He glanced around at the various faces as the mockery of a trial continued.

He had no idea what had really happened. He was sure only that he had not shot Jenks in the back. But someone had. Who?

Slocum's brain was still fuzzy. His head wound looked worse than it was. The war club had struck a glancing blow, but had opened up the scalp. Emily had cleaned it well, though, and it would heal. He did not even feel the slight wound in his thigh. The death of the Bryant boy still weighed on him. He felt badly about Pearl. His fault. He should have been more careful. The men here should have been taking care of that instead of trying him illegally. There was only one way, of course—go after her. But that was impossible to do with Rossiter and Shoop drawing down on him and the hours taken up with this farce of a trial.

"I think we should take him into custody and turn him over to Captain Scott," Nellie Loving was saying.

"And I say," Emily Schoolcraft spoke up, "that he didn't do it. He was asleep all night."

"Reckon I'd have to disagree with you, ma'am," Rossiter said with broad, almost courtly respect. "I'd say he had to have done it. It was his gun and it was still warm from firing when we found it. Then, what with Mrs. Loving telling us about Slocum's past..." The gunfighter shook his head sadly as if the last thing he wanted to do in the world was pick on poor John Slocum.

Throughout this exchange, Slocum kept his eyes on Lee Dimmock. The man was nervous, fidgety. What was he hiding?

Emily spoke up again. "I wouldn't have trusted Mr. Jenks to ever tell the truth unless it benefited him in some way."

"Not polite to speak of the dead that way," Nellie Loving said.

"I think it's a good idea, for the safety of everybody, if we bind his hands and keep him strapped down in one of the wagons," said Shoop.

The big, slow-moving Texan spoke with the calm and purposefulness of a minister. Again there was the impression that the last thing he wanted to do was harm a decent man like Slocum.

"I mean, there's women along, and we should protect them," Shoop said. "Then when we get to Virginia City, we can let him be tried by a real judge and jury."

"Sounds reasonable to me," Rossiter put in. He and Shoop exchanged glances. It was a long way to Virginia City. Anything could happen.

"He's not a criminal," Jennie said angrily. "He was too sick to shoot Jenks. He wasn't even awake."

"Seems you have a vested interest in helping him," Nellie Loving snapped.

"And seems you have a vested interest in hurting him," Jennie said.

Slocum sat there glumly, his head aching, his senses alive to the sparkling early autumn day.

These kinds of hours should be spent with a hunting dog and a good rifle searching for pheasant or quail, not sitting here and—

A movement caught Slocum's eye. Alvin and Raymond, off to themselves, suddenly rose up, weapons in their hands.

Raymond leveled a double-barreled Greener at Rossiter. Alvin covered Shoop with a similar scattergun.

"Drop your gunbelts, gentlemans," said Raymond, his voice deadly calm.

The pair did as they were told. The rigs made a sound as they hit the dirt.

"Alvin, what in God's name are you doing?" Nellie Loving screeched. "It's not bad enough that you try to thwart justice, now you've gone and thrown in with a nigger."

"I decided it's high time I be a man," Alvin said. "If none of the rest of you will stick up for Slocum here, then I damned sure will."

"Then be a man," Nellie beseeched. "Go back with me and take over my father's business and become the mayor. You can even be governor some day."

Raymond said dourly, "Untie his hands."

Rossiter gave the black man a contemptuous look. "Nigger, you're really gonna regret this."

Raymond gestured with his shotgun.

Grimly, Rossiter complied. Slocum stood, groggily.

"Well, now," he said. "Maybe we can do what we ought to do. Go after Pearl. Loving, you catch up three horses. I can use you and Raymond. Jennie, can you get us some grub? Beef jerky, hardtack, nothing heavy. Nothing that will make noise." He picked up the gunbelts, slung them over his shoulder. His own gunbelt lay atop a barrel keg. He strapped it on and reloaded.

Alvin Loving nodded and went after the horses.

"Will you be all right?" Slocum asked Emily.

"These people don't scare me," she said bravely. "The folks in St. Louis were a lot meaner." She smiled, raked a scathing glance over Nellie Loving, Rossiter, and Shoop. "And smarter too."

Slocum said, "We're going to find Pearl."

"I'm saying prayers," Emily said.

To Rossiter, Slocum said, "You hurt her, I'll kill you."

Rossiter had the good sense to say nothing.

Alvin brought up three horses. Slocum smiled. One was his own. The other two belonged to the Texans.

Slocum tossed pistols to Alvin and Raymond. He checked his single cinch, mounted up. Jennie stuffed dry grub in their saddlebags. Each man carried his bedroll tied behind the cantle of his saddle. Emily brought him his hat. He put it on gingerly and saluted.

"We'll be back," he said. "Be careful."

He rode out, followed by the two men he had chosen to go with him.

"You came up with those shotguns at the right time," he told Loving. "How?"

"You know how it is with slaves," said Alvin, his tone tinged with irony. "Nobody pays us much attention."

For the next few hours the three men followed the Bozeman Trail, Slocum tracking, following the path made by unshod ponies' hooves.

The mountains towered against the cobalt sky. The short grasses thatched an earth already firm from cold.

The bracing air cleared out the cobwebs in Slocum's brain.

They paused several times before nightfall to give their horses a rest.

They rode on into the dying day, until the sky was a smear of clouds painted red and yellow.

The sun sank over the western peaks. Slocum pointed to a stream trickling out of a foothill canyon.

"We'll stay the night there," he said. "No fire. Pull on some jerky, dry biscuits, if you get hungry."

Leather creaked as the men dismounted. The stream gurgled. Slocum saw the moccasin tracks, said nothing. Moments later, Raymond let out a sound.

"Looky there," he said.

Slocum and Loving both saw it.

Part of woman's dress, hanging like a tattered flag from the branch of an alder bush.

"That Pearl's?" asked Loving.

Slocum nodded grimly.

He looked around, listened. He knelt down, looked at the tracks in the soft mud of the creek bank. Water filled them. Not all the way. The muddy edges were blurred. How long? he wondered. Two hours? Closer to three. The two men watched him, holding on to the reins of their horses.

John stood up, took in a breath.

"They stopped here on purpose," he said. "Three hours ago. They're not in any big hurry."

"Maybe they're still here," said Loving, a slight quaver in his voice.

"No, they're gone. But they meant for us to know they were here. They left that," Slocum pointed to the fragment torn from Pearl's dress, "to keep us interested."

"What does you mean?" asked Raymond, his eyes

white in their sockets.

"It means," said Slocum, "that we can expect to run into them up the trail somewhere."

"Where? When?" asked Loving, the quaver quite pronounced now.

"Oh," Slocum said casually, "when we least expect to see them, I reckon."

10

Slocum took the last shift, woke the men up before day-break. They were in their saddles as dawn cracked the sky over the eastern horizon. They picked up the trail as soon as it was light enough to see. Alvin and Raymond held up well for tenderfeet. He did not push them. The Sioux were traveling fast now, and he figured they were a good half day's ride ahead of them. They were not yet hiding their tracks. For long miles the three men rode. In the distance, lining the foothills, deep stands of ponderosa pine and Douglas fir rose in tiers to timberline. A fresh dusting of snow blanketed the lower mountains. The higher mountain peaks were lost in haze, the thick cotton of clouds.

Near midday, the men stopped.

"Take fifteen minutes," said Slocum. "Any more and you're liable to stiffen up."

Slocum chewed on jerky, sniffed the air. His strength was returning, the wounds healing under scabs.

"Wonder how Nellie's doing," Alvin Loving said abruptly.

Slocum couldn't imagine anybody actually missing

that woman. Not because she was so horrible-looking—
he'd seen much worse in frontier towns—but because
her personality was so belligerent and unyielding. He'd
never seen her act kind or charitable for a moment. Never
once had he seen her smile about anything. And he
couldn't forget the lies she'd told about him, a supposed
rape and murder charge in Ohio. Even if Jenks had told
her, she had to take responsibility for spreading false
testimony about him. Many people had lied about Slocum
in his days.

"Let's mount up," said Slocum.

They had gone two or three more miles when they
saw an unlikely sight. Slocum reined up.

There in the middle of the prairie a medicine wagon
rolled and jostled. Pull the flap down in the back and
you'd have a stage for a gent in a top hat and undertaker's
outfit to sell you all kinds of elixirs, the chief aim of
which was to make your heart beat stronger, your life
run longer, and your aches and pains go away.

"What the hell?" Raymond said.

Slocum shrugged. "There's a feller who may be more
lost than we are."

"Yeah," Alvin said. "Or else they're still chasin' him
from the last town and he decided Indians are safer than
dissatisfied customers."

They spurred their horses and caught up with the
wagon, a Springfield with bric-a-brac and gingerbread
decorations gussying it up. On both sides, in careful
circus script, was painted PROFESSOR DION'S HEALTH
WAGON.

The gent driving the wagon looked as if he were in
need of his own elixir. He had eyes that shone with some
sort of disease—Slocum suspected the sort that came

from a moonshine bottle—and teeth stained as yellow as fool's gold. His body was bent and cadaverous and predictably garbed in the kind of motheaten fancy-dan tails and stovepipe hat that only served to point up the man's poverty. The horses that pulled the cart were lucky to be pulling anything. Flop-eared, dry-nosed, their backs sagging like barrel staves, the animals were as wretched as the wagon itself.

Professor Dion pulled the team to a stop and looked up at Slocum. "I trust you didn't come to rob me, sir," he said in a voice laden with the sepulchral resonance of a stage actor.

Slocum suppressed a smile. What would he take from this old coot? His set of fine horses? A few cases of an elixir that would do little more than get you drunk and give you the trots next day?

"No, sir," Slocum said. "I surely didn't come to rob you."

"Did you see any Sioux?" asked Alvin.

Professor Dion peered through ancient eyes at the three men and cleared his throat. "Unfortunately I saw some last night." A nervous tic started across his face. "They spared my life but they diminished my supply of elixir, I'm afraid." He smiled with his terrible teeth. "Somewhere over there are a bunch of Indians who are enjoying themselves a great deal, I dare say."

"We're looking for Red Cloud," Slocum said.

Professor Dion's face grew serious. "You look for Red Cloud? I'm told it's usually the other way around. He looks for the white man—and finds him." He scratched at a place just beneath his threadbare stovepipe hat. "But it's Running Moon I thought you'd be interested in. He's been on the warpath lately. I'm told that he is becoming an enemy of Red Cloud, a challenger to Red Cloud's power."

Slocum had his first suspicions about the man just then. Much of the stage English disappeared, as did the slurred, liquory words. He spoke confidently and impressively about the state of Indian affairs. Slocum wondered who the man really was and what he was doing out here.

Their conversation was interrupted then by the bark of a rifle close by.

Slocum brought a hand to his forehead to block the sun from his eyes. Even with the Stetson's brim shading his eyes, the late afternoon light was brilliant.

Half a dozen painted Sioux sat their ponies a quarter of a mile away, watching.

"Lord," said Alvin Loving.

His word sounded very much like a prayer.

"Would you mind if I put in with you for the evening?" Professor Dion said. "I have a feeling it could be a very long night and that we'll need every man we can get."

From the floor he lifted a shotgun and showed it to Slocum.

"Welcome aboard, Professor," Slocum said.

Around a fire that danced off the side of his painted wagon, Professor Dion sat and told tales of scientific marvels that amused all three of his listeners, though not one of them believed a word he said.

The sweet smell of pine mingled with the aroma of beans and salt pork the Professor had offered the men.

The horses grazed, whickered softly as they fed.

Slocum sat on his bedroll, out of the firelight, never looking directly into its flames, listening.

He was still having serious doubts about the Professor and wondered exactly what he was doing wandering around out here. The man had not mentioned Captain Scott or the Bozeman Trail or anything specific about where he'd been or where in hell he was going.

Raymond and Alvin listened to the drummer intently as Dion spoke of everything under the sun except himself.

"Where have you spent your time?" Slocum asked when the right moment came in the conversation.

"My time, sir?" Professor Dion asked stagily. "Why, I've spent my time in the intellectual circles of the world."

"Where were you coming from when we met up with you?"

The Professor snorted. "Why, from Nebraska, sir."

Slocum smiled. "One of the intellectual circles of the world?"

"Are you making fun of me?"

"No. But I am trying to figure you out."

"That's been tried before," the Professor said tightly. "By many, many people. Just let me say that I elude knowing in many respects. I am a complicated man."

Slocum decided to be even more direct. "Why aren't you on the Bozeman Trail?"

Professor Dion's eyes narrowed. "Because, like you, I presume, the good Captain Scott forbade my traveling it. The road is closed, sir."

Captain Scott again. Slocum decided that because of all the events of the past few days, maybe he was being overly suspicious. Maybe the Professor here was just who and what he seemed.

Raymond said, "Who's taking the first watch?"

"I shall, if you desire, sir," Professor Dion said.

"Fine," Slocum said, his head starting to ache again.

Then, "You never finished telling us about Running Moon."

The Professor shook his head. "A madman. I've seen what he's done to poor white travelers. At least Red Cloud is something of a politician in his own way. By killing, he's simply trying to gain some bargaining power for his people. He needs to keep both the whites and the redskins with him, as it were. He can't afford to go in for outright atrocity because he knows that Washington will not deal with him then." He shook his head again. In the firelight there was a comic aspect to the man in his stovepipe hat. "Running Moon feels no such constraint. He seems to symbolize all the hatred and frustration that the red man feels deep in his heart. I dare say I've seen my share of savagery out here as I've traveled around, but I've never seen a redskin as vicious as Running Moon."

As he spoke, Slocum thought about his drovers, including the Bryant boy, who'd been slaughtered the other evening. He thought of how they'd been disemboweled, how they'd been scalped.

"As a matter of fact, right now it's said that Red Cloud wants to stop Running Moon as bad as the white man does," Professor Dion said. "Running Moon has his own group of braves and they do what they choose. Red Cloud can neither find him nor control him."

The more the Professor talked, the more convinced Slocum became that the man he was looking for—both to avenge the deaths of his drovers and to get Pearl back—was not Red Cloud, after all, but Running Moon.

He could see that Raymond was thinking the same thing.

The black man sat next to the fire, holding his shotgun,

rocking back and forth to some inner rhythm. From the bitter way he stared into the fire, it was easy to imagine what he was thinking about.

The same thing Slocum was thinking about.

How good it would feel to kill Running Moon.

Slocum drew the third watch that night. The overcast moon soaked the land in silver, the mountains no more than a smudge against the skyline. Slocum stood well beyond the horses, the Professor's wagon, and the sleeping men.

When the sound came he was not surprised. He held perfectly still, invisible in the shadows.

The Sioux crawled snakelike from behind a huge boulder some fifty yards away.

Slocum heard him coming, a rasping against the sandy soil and the dead autumn grasses.

The Indian stood up. Moccasins whispered through the seared grasses.

Slocum drew his knife, waited.

The brave started running toward Slocum. Slocum moved, then, into his path. The Indian lunged toward the white man.

His hands, one of which wielded a knife, reached for Slocum's throat.

John threw up an arm, twisted under the Indian's charge. He brought his own knife up, slashed at the red man's wrist. The blade struck flesh, slid into bone. The warrior made no sound. Slocum wrapped an arm around the Indian's neck, brought a knee up hard into the man's back. Slocum threw the brave to the ground, ground his face into the earth.

The brave writhed and moaned as Slocum drew the

man's arm back, put all of his weight onto the small of the back. He put his knife to the Indian's throat, panted for breath.

He could easily have sliced the man's head from his shoulders. But he knew there was more than one Indian. He released the man's arm, drew his pistol. He slashed downward, cracking the Indian's skull with the butt of his weapon. The Indian slumped into unconsciousness.

When the next brave appeared from behind the boulder, Slocum was ready for him.

Still kneeling atop the first brave, Slocum raised his pistol, hammered it back to cock, and shot away the second brave's face.

The camp came to life. Slocum heard Alvin scream out in terror.

Two other braves emerged from the darkness and raced toward Slocum.

"Watch out," said Slocum. "The other side."

He heard the clatter of shotguns cracking open, the rattle of shells being slammed into chambers.

"Here they come!" yelled Raymond.

Professor Dion clambered from his wagon, a wraith in white longjohns, a shotgun in his hands.

Slocum fired twice more, when the Indians were right on top of him. He watched them stagger and fall. One skidded close, his chest pumping blood through a black hole.

Alvin Loving ran up to Slocum and said, "Let me kill one, all right?"

"Christ," said Slocum.

He wheeled, saw a brave streak toward the black man. Raymond's shotgun exploded orange fire and lead. The brave fell dead, his chest and stomach leaking like a bloody sieve.

Loving gasped. His eyes glittered. "Did you do that?" he murmured.

Slocum twisted his neck, looking for another Indian.

"Here he comes," said Dion, bringing his shotgun to his shoulder. He pulled both triggers.

The brave rushing toward them out of the shadows danced as the lead pellets ripped through flesh and muscles, struck vital organs. He looked, for a moment, like a puppet on the end of a string.

There was an obscene grace in the way his arms flew out from his body, almost as if they weren't attached to the torso. His head snapped back until the spine cracked. He died in a bloody heap.

"Damn," Alvin Loving said happily. "He's dead, isn't he?"

"Can't get no deader than that," Raymond said.

There was one more. Slocum saw him crawling silently toward them as the moon came from behind a cloud. He saw only the feathers at first, thicker than the grasses, then the glint of his rifle in the now clear moonlight.

Slocum fired once, missed. The brave leaped to his feet and charged. Slocum fired his last shot, struck the Indian in the forearm. The rifle clattered as it struck the ground. The Indian drew his knife.

Then the dance began.

The death dance.

Slocum and the brave stalked each other, circled each other slowly.

Dion, Alvin, and Raymond watched, their eyes fixed in bright stares.

Slocum holstered his empty pistol and shifted his Bowie knife to his right hand.

The two men closed, grappled. Blades flashed, arced

through the air. The whishing sound was like a whispering breeze.

The Sioux brave broke free, began to sing his death song.

"It is a good day to die," he chanted, in the Ogalalla tongue. "All of my life is around me and I am full..."

The back of Slocum's neck crawled. The white man went into a crouch, stalked in, holding his knife low. He thrust upward, twisted away as the Sioux's blade knifed downward. He felt his blade-tip rake across ribs, part soft flesh.

The warrior grunted and broke off his song. He lunged for Slocum.

John let him come on, stepped aside at the last moment. He rammed hard with his Bowie, aiming for the Indian's exposed flank.

The knife sank home. Slocum gave it a quick twist.

The brave's legs crumpled, his knees buckled. The man grasped at the knife jutting from his side. Blood oozed from the ruptured flesh. He struggled to rise from his knees, grasped the handle of the blade. He tried to pull it free, but his fingers slipped off, slick with blood.

Alvin Loving stood with the rest of the men, watching fascinated.

"I—I never saw anything like this," he said.

The brave slumped to the ground. Most of the bleeding was inside, Slocum knew. He drew his pistol, began to reload. There was no use in a man suffering like that. He worked the ejector, kicking out the empty hulls. The brave watched him, his eyes dull in the moonlight.

Slocum took a breath.

"White Eyes good man," said the Sioux in English. Then his eyes frosted over with the glaze of death. He expelled a last breath, slumped into his final sleep.

• • •

The first Indian was alive. Slocum slapped him back to consciousness and looked into his sullen, painted face.

"I want you to lead me to your camp," he said slowly, "or I will kill you."

The hell of it was, he could see that the brave did not understand—at least not exactly—what he was talking about.

Professor Dion stepped forward. He stood over the Indian and made several quick, deft signs with his fingers.

The brave grunted and signed back.

"What does he say?" asked Slocum.

"He says he'll take us to Running Moon," Professor Dion said.

"All right," said Slocum. "Fix him up. Alvin, you and Raymond see if you can't catch up a pony for this one to ride."

The two men hesitated, saw the hard look in Slocum's eyes, and tramped off to do what he had told them to do.

Slocum fixed the medicine drummer with a look.

Dion lowered his eyes.

Something was wrong here. The brave had agreed to take them to Running Moon, wherever he was. It was too easy.

Slocum wondered why.

11

The coyote, no more than a gray shadow, slunk through the grasses, avoiding the strange procession that had robbed it of a rabbit it had been stalking.

The captive Indian, whom the Professor informed the others was named Tall Bear because of his height, sat next to Dion on the wagon as it rolled and jarred over the rough prairie. His hands and ankles were bound together. The Indian ponies had run off before Raymond or Alvin could capture them.

Several times they had to stop to fix one of the wheels that had come loose. At one such stop, the brave tried to jump from the wagon. Raymond slugged the Indian and shoved him back up on the seat.

"Next time I'll use this," said the black man, brandishing the Greener. The buck glowered at him.

Dion pursed his lips and said nothing.

Slocum made a note to keep an eye on both the brave and the drummer.

They crossed Crazy Woman Creek, tracked into the low foothills of the Big Horns. The silence grew up around them, eerie as a graveyard.

Slocum could almost smell Sioux.

The others were nervous too, except for the Indian, who sat the seat like a stone.

The tracks now were fresh. Tall Bear watched Slocum with narrowed eyes as the big man threaded his horse over the wide trail, his rifle laid across the pommel.

Slocum almost missed it.

The road took a bend, and he was halfway into it when he saw something move. He ducked and turned his mount to warn the others.

Alvin Loving's horse took the arrow in the flank, staggering under the driving weight of the shaft.

The horse screamed, bucked, and kicked in agony. Alvin Loving screeched along with him. He lost his seating, hit the ground in a crash of bones and flesh.

Slocum brought his rifle to his shoulder.

"Pull that wagon up and set the brake!" Slocum yelled to Professor Dion. To Alvin and Raymond, he said, "Use the wagon for cover. Get underneath. Take that Indian down with you."

Less than two minutes later, the four men were lying beneath the wagon, firing rifles and shotguns at four Sioux who were less than a hundred yards away.

Tall Bear's face was a bronzed mask. Yet something flickered in his eyes, something that caught Slocum's attention.

At first Slocum reasoned that this was because the brave thought he was about to be rescued and was merely excited. But soon he saw that the Indian was frightened.

"What the hell's wrong with him?" Slocum asked Professor Dion above the explosions of gunfire. "The son of a bitch should be celebrating."

Professor Dion set his rifle down and crawled on his

elbows over to Tall Bear.

He spoke with the Indian for a few minutes and then crawled back to Slocum. Tall Bear's eyes widened. He appeared to be greatly agitated.

"What's going on?" Slocum asked, taking aim. Thus far none of the four braves charging them had been so much as grazed.

Raymond fumbled with a pair of shotshells. His rattled nerves showed in the way his fingers shook as he tried to reload.

Loving fired blindly and missed.

"He's afraid he's going to be captured," Professor Dion explained.

Slocum smiled bitterly. "He's afraid. What about us?"

"He says these are Red Cloud's braves and that they consider him their enemy. He says he will be tortured to death if they get him."

"He's probably right. We could expect the same."

"Tall Bear wants to die like a man, not tied up. He is genuinely afraid of being captured."

"I guess you weren't exaggerating about the split between Red Cloud and Running Moon."

"Not in the least."

Slocum got off a shot, a good one. One of the Indians crumpled, skidded on his chest and stomach, blood spurting from his neck. He quivered for several moments, then lay still.

A few minutes later Alvin Loving got lucky. He dropped a brave who'd been coming in from the side. He croaked with joy and raised his Greener overhead in a victory gesture.

"Settle down, Loving," said Slocum. "You drew blood, but it's not over with yet."

"Two more," said Raymond, as he closed the breech.

His voice quavered, but he was over the shakes.

Slocum flashed him a wry smile. "Cover the right flank, Raymond," said the big man. "Dion, you watch our rear. Loving, you watch that left flank."

"What about you?" asked Loving.

"I'm going to draw them out," he said. "Cover me and the redskin."

He crawled over to Tall Bear.

"Sorry," Slocum said, "but I'm going to have to use you as bait."

He dragged the Indian by his shirt over to the side of the wagon. He propped Tall Bear up in plain and easy sight, just long enough to get the two remaining attackers burned up enough to come after the renegade Indian.

One of the Sioux brought his rifle up to his shoulder. Quickly, Slocum pulled Tall Bear back down, just as the rifle cracked. A lead ball slammed into the wagon's side.

Tall Bear glowered at Slocum.

"You're going up there again," said the white man tightly, "until they get so mad they'll come at us."

Slocum stood the Indian up again. This time, both Sioux fired at once, and Slocum barely got Tall Bear back down out of danger. He heard the actions of the two Sharps as the Sioux jacked open the receivers. He wondered if they would waste another couple of shots at Tall Bear. Probably not.

"Get set," Slocum told the others. He cocked his rifle and waited.

The Sioux disappeared.

"They're gone," said Raymond.

"Don't you bet on it," said Slocum.

One of the Sioux came in from Slocum's left flank. The other darted in from the right, hunched over, running on silent moccasins.

The first shot was true enough that Raymond nearly got his head taken off. A huge chunk of the wagon maybe two inches from his skull exploded from one of their bullets. The Sioux fell flat and reloaded before Slocum could get off a shot. The one charging from his left gave out a war whoop, brought his rifle up.

Slocum shot him in the throat at close range.

The Indian's momentum carried him forward so that Slocum had to roll away. Blood gushed from his throat. Tall Bear stared at the dying warrior, his eyes glittering like agates.

Slocum started scanning for the other brave. It grew quiet, except for the gurgling rattle in the dying brave's throat. It was an ugly death. Alvin watched the Indian in abject fascination. The sight of the Indian dying that way seemed to weigh heavy on Alvin Loving.

"God," he whimpered under his breath. His face went pale.

He had come a long way from the henpecked husband in just a few short days, Slocum thought.

Suddenly Raymond shouted. "Oh, Lord, here he come!"

"Shoot him," said Slocum.

Dion twisted his body, swung his rifle.

Raymond got off both barrels of the Greener. The brave seemed to stop dead in his tracks, hang motionless for several seconds as blood flowed from a dozen wounds. His waist looked like a sieve. Then the Indian convulsed and pitched forward. The brave under the wagon shook his leg twice in a last reflex. His eyes frosted over and remained fixed in a terrible empty stare.

Slocum stood up and looked at Raymond. "You cut that buck near clean in two," said the big man as he looked at the dead Sioux.

"Yes, sir, for what they done to my wife."

Slocum nodded, turned away from Raymond's half-mad eyes. He had seen that look before, during the War, in men who had tasted their first blood.

That night, Professor Dion said, "Have you ever seen a ghost, Mr. Slocum?"

Slocum, his belly full, tiredness seeping through his muscles, lit his quirly from the campfire and said, "Not that I can remember." He grinned. "At least not sober."

Raymond had drawn first watch. Alvin Loving was already asleep. Tall Bear was bound to the wagon wheel.

"I did a little investigating into the matter," the Professor said loftily, "and I concluded that they actually do exist. Only not, perhaps, as we think of them."

"I don't think of them much."

"I'd say each of you must believe in ghosts," the Professor said.

"Why's that?"

"Because each of you, in his way, seems to be haunted. Running from something. You can see it in your faces."

Slocum hated this kind of talk. "I'm a little tired, Professor." He closed his eyes to make sure Dion would get his point.

"I just like to know a little something about the people I travel with, is all," the Professor said.

"I guess I could say the same thing."

All the Professor had explained so far was that Captain Scott had kept him off the Bozeman Trail and that his destination was Virginia City.

"You'd like to know more about me?" the drummer asked.

"Yes."

"I'm afraid I'm not very interesting."

"I doubt that, Professor."

The man still wore his stovepipe hat. In the campfire light he managed to look ludicrous and sinister at the same time.

"A poor ham actor is all," the Professor said, "reduced to making a living by selling elixirs to rubes."

As he listened to the man talk, Slocum, despite his tiredness, knew what he was going to do.

He would have to put off sleep for a while.

The Professor had the next watch.

Raymond came off watch and went to sleep immediately.

Slocum had been pretending to be asleep for the last twenty minutes.

The Professor picked up his weapon and went out into the night.

Slocum got up quickly.

Tall Bear slumped in slumber. Slocum had to be careful not to wake him. Since Tall Bear and the Professor spoke the same language, Tall Bear, out of perversity, might tell the old man what Slocum had done.

Slocum eased himself up into the wagon, opened the small door leading inside, and disappeared into the waiting darkness.

The interior stank of the elixir, part alcohol, part herbs.

After ten minutes of poking around, he found nothing more than drawings of the Professor in various foppish poses from theatrical roles.

In one corner of the wagon he saw a trunk. He had just started to raise the lid when he heard a noise from outside. Before he had time to move, the wagon door opened and there stood Professor Dion.

The man must have had the eyes of a mountain lion, because even in the gloom he spotted Slocum easily.

"May I ask, sir," he intoned, "what you are doing in the wagon I rightly and legally own?"

"I needed some of your elixir," Slocum said lamely. "I was taking a chill. I thought it might warm me up." When cornered, he reasoned, get off the defensive; attack. "Anyway, why did you come back? Your watch can't be over yet."

The Professor smiled sarcastically. "Let's just call it a coincidence. I, too, was taking a chill and felt the need for some of my elixir."

"I think that drummer man's leading us in circles," Raymond said at mid-morning the next day.

By now Tall Bear's directions were becoming highly suspicious. Where exactly would they find Running Moon?

Left up to Tall Bear, Slocum thought, the answer was probably nowhere.

Slocum grabbed the reins of the wagon team, brought his own mount up to the wagon, and then grabbed Tall Bear from his perch, pulling the brave to the ground.

Tall Bear looked up at the white man with ill-concealed malice. Slocum dismounted and stood head-to-head with the Indian.

"Dion," said Slocum, "you tell this buck that I haven't read any sign in the last hour. If he wants to go on living, he'd better point us in the right direction. If we get jumped, I'll cut his throat."

Dion spoke in rapid, guttural Lakota.

Slocum drew his Bowie knife for emphasis.

Tall Bear spoke, moved his head so that he nodded toward an entirely different direction.

"He says that soon we will pick up the trail again. He says he does not lie."

"When will we catch up to Running Moon? Ask him that."

After some talk, Dion translated.

"By the time the moon comes up," he says, "we will be close to his camp on Clear Creek. That's not far. Half a day's ride."

"Do you believe him?" asked Slocum.

Dion shrugged.

"Maybe. I don't think Tall Bear's afraid of you, though."

"No, I suppose not. Tell him his life is hanging on a short string." Slocum sheathed the Bowie, stepped back up in the saddle. He watched as Dion finished translating.

"Now, get his ass back up in the wagon and let's move," said the big man.

Tall Bear smirked as Dion helped him back up on the seat.

A short time later, Slocum saw pony tracks. They crossed a fork of Clear Creek toward nightfall. The pony tracks were fresher now, and Slocum thought that perhaps Tall Bear had told the truth. As the land turned smoky with the twilight of dusk, he led his party up the second branch of the creek, still following the pony tracks.

"We'll make camp here," he said softly, reining up. "Dry. No fire. No noise."

Later, after they had all eaten jerky and hardtack, Slocum told Dion to get the Indian ready to walk.

"I want to see that camp," he said.

Dion translated.

"He says it's very close. There is a valley up past the next rise. That is where they'll be."

"How does he know that?"

"He knows. Smell it?" Dion sniffed. Slocum did the same. Woodsmoke, the barest trace of it on the night air.

"We all go," he said. "Bring ammunition. Leave everything else here."

Ten minutes later they were climbing the slope. The smell of smoke was stronger now. As they cleared the summit, Slocum saw the glow of firelight in the night sky. They walked to the edge, looked down into the valley below.

Slocum estimated that there could be as many as two hundred Indians.

This was not an Indian village with women and children to do the work. This was a camp of warriors.

Close, no more than four hundred yards away, where the creek made a bend as it cut a path from the high peaks.

From the largest teepee came a beefy man in a rawhide outfit that seemed to be half-Sioux and half-white man's trading post. He wore a hat with a feather in it and white man's boots.

Slocum pointed to the man. "Ask Tall Bear if that's the renegade," Slocum said to Dion.

"No need to. You're looking at the man you've been tracking."

Slocum sucked in a breath. Yes, this was Running Moon, fiercest of the Sioux warriors.

Then Slocum felt a shock tingle all the way up his spine and explode in his head.

From the same teepee where Running Moon had come another person now appeared, a woman whose clothes had been clawed and ripped until she was virtually naked, her sensuous, full-breasted body on display for all to see.

As he had figured, by finding Running Moon he had also found Pearl.

Raymond looked away quickly.

Alvin said, "Probably not a lot left of her from the way she appears."

Slocum shook his head bitterly. "I figure some of those bucks put the boots to her all right. Damn."

Raymond hefted his shotgun. "If we was close," he said, "I could fix him so he couldn't do nothing to her ever again."

Alvin Loving moved closer. "There's a lot of them."

"That there is," Slocum said.

"You got any plans?" Professor Dion asked.

Slocum did not smile. "Not a one."

12

"You ever see so many Indians all at once't?" Raymond asked Alvin Loving.

"No," Loving whispered.

Slocum knew they had to back off, give some thought about the best way to rescue Pearl. The longer they stayed here, the more chance there was that they would be discovered. He motioned for them to follow him. He led them downslope, then found a place where they could wait until the camp quieted down.

"We'll set a spell," he said. "You want to talk, talk. But keep it low."

The men did what comes natural to men when they had nothing else to talk about.

Alvin Loving began discussing all the nights he'd spent with whores.

At first, Raymond and Dion, because Alvin was not exactly their idea of a he-man, discounted his exploits. But soon they saw that he was telling the truth and that he recounted his adventures in an interesting way.

Even Slocum, who was thinking hard about the best

way to free Pearl, began to pay more than passing interest to the man's tales of his prowess with women.

"There was this one named Ramona," Alvin said. "She wanted to meet some better-paying customers, so she started going to the church Nellie and I attended. Well, one night after choir practice, I was up in the loft. The church was very dark. Out of the shadows came this Ramona, you see.

"She wore a proper gingham dress, the only difference being that the front of it swelled way out with her breasts. I couldn't take my eyes off them. Finally, I asked if I could walk her home, it being late and no time for ladies to be strolling. She said she would appreciate it.

"Several times on the way home little 'accidents' kept happening. Her hand kept finding excuses to brush up against my crotch. Remember now, I had no idea she was a whore. I thought she was a fine upstanding church-woman. But she was driving me crazy anyway.

"So we got to her house and who should appear on the steps but a blond girl who was just as shapely as Ramona. Before I could leave they put their heads together and whispered something and then invited me inside. They kept giggling the whole time.

"The reason they invited me in was to help them learn some new hymns, which I was glad to show them. They had a piano and I started to sing. But before I got very far into the song, Ramona came over and dropped to her knees and started sucking me off. I tried to keep on singing, but it was no use. Then the blonde came over. She opened her blouse and slid my hand inside. She had great big soft tits with very hard little nipples. Then she took my other hand and put it up inside her and then she really started working away while all the time Ramona kept doing me up.

"We all ended up in a bed upstairs where they took turns with me. It was really something, let me tell you."

The Professor, Raymond, and even the Indian seemed transfixed by Alvin's tale.

All Slocum said was, "I'm sure glad you told us that story."

"Why's that?"

"Because it gave me an idea."

"About how we're going into the camp?"

"Yeah."

"How?"

"It's like the two girls you talked about," Slocum said. "We'll send two Indians down there. Tall Bear and one more."

"But there's only one Indian."

"Pretty soon there's going to be two," Slocum said.

Back at their camp, Slocum took Tall Bear's shirt from him and rubbed a goodly amount of dirt over his face. He saddled two horses.

He had taken the precaution of stuffing a rag deep into Tall Bear's mouth so that if the brave tried to scream he would end up choking himself.

"Tell him," Slocum said to Dion, "that if he makes one bad move, he'll catch a lead ball in his back."

The Indian said nothing as he listened to Dion's words. He sat stolidly in the saddle atop Raymond's horse. His hands and feet were untied.

"Be ready to leave in a hurry, and shoot whoever's chasing us when we come back," Slocum told the men.

"You don't want us to help?" asked Raymond.

"The two of us might get in there, get the girl out. I figure they'll spy Tall Bear here first, and give me the time I need."

"You're either brave or a fool," said Dion.

Loving drew a breath and shook his head in disbelief.

Slocum prodded Tall Bear to lead out. The two men rode up the hill, Tall Bear in front, Slocum right behind him with pistol drawn.

As he had planned, they rode right into Running Moon's camp. Several braves ran forward to greet Tall Bear.

Slocum shoved the Indian off his horse, then whipped his own animal into action. He rode for the lodge where he had seen Pearl earlier. The two bucks, taken by surprise as his horse galloped toward them, danced out of the way. Neither was armed.

Running Moon came out of his lodge. He had Pearl in front of him as a shield. He carried a warclub in his free hand.

Slocum charged straight for the two.

"Run, Pearl!" he said.

Pearl, groggy from her ordeal, glanced up at the man on horseback, her eyes wide with fright. Running Moon raised his warclub. Pearl broke away. As he rode in close, Slocum leaned over and encircled her waist. He hauled her into the saddle as he stood up in the stirrups, slid his butt back up the cantle. He jerked her roughly up on his lap and swung the horse in a circle as Running Moon threw his warclub. The weapon hissed through the air, narrowly missing Slocum's skull.

The Indian camp erupted in a frenzy of gunfire and curses and screams. War cries filled the air.

Braves in hideous warpaint rushed toward him, their white man's rifles spitting flame in the night.

Slocum fired at shadowy figures, bent low in the saddle, forcing Pearl over the saddlehorn, covering her with his body.

Bullets fried the air over his head. He spurred his horse away from the camp, heading for the slope that would take him and Pearl out of the valley.

That was when he saw them.

The caravan of Professor Dion's wagon and Dion, Raymond, and Alvin Loving walking with their hands on top of their heads, prisoner-style, while at least half a dozen braves jabbed at them with rifles.

A scouting party must have discovered their camp about the time that Slocum and Tall Bear had left. Slocum let out a curse and hauled in on the reins.

He halted his horse as one of the braves, seeing him, put the muzzle of his rifle right next to Raymond's ear.

Slocum knew that if he wanted Raymond to live, he would have to lay down his own weapon.

Pearl, hysterical, turned in the saddle and sobbed into Slocum's chest, "Please take me out of here."

"Looks like we're not going any farther," he said.

"You don't know what they've been doing to me."

"I can imagine," Slocum said.

He holstered his pistol and waited for the Indians to come for him.

Two burly, painted braves grabbed Slocum's arms. They pulled him from his horse and threw him violently to the ground. Wild whoops filled the air. Jubilant Sioux raced up to the prisoners and cried out in glee.

A hard foot slammed Slocum in the stomach.

He was rolling away from the next blow when he saw Running Moon. The warrior stood to the right of him, his body bronze in the firelight. A knife glinted in one hand. In the other was a Colt, its hammer cocked.

"You boss here?" Running Moon asked in thick, accented English.

Slocum did not know what to say. Only a few days

ago he'd been driving five hundred head of longhorns to Virginia City.

He shrugged.

Running Moon kicked him in the groin.

Slocum doubled over in pain. His senses whirled. Bile rose up in his throat and he gagged, struggling for air.

Around him the Sioux started to laugh.

Running Moon lashed out with his foot again, this time catching Slocum in the ribs.

Slocum no longer knew where to grab, which part of his body hurt worst.

The Sioux laughed again as Slocum vomited.

The kicks and the vomiting and the scorn were only the beginning.

The prisoners were taken to the center of the ring of teepees, where a big fire blazed. Braves struck them, pulled their hair, thudded fists into their stomachs. They taunted the black man in Lakota, knocked him to his knees twice before they lined the prisoners up.

Slocum saw the Indians form two rows, just wide enough apart to allow a man to pass. A pair of warriors tied Pearl to crossed lodgepoles used to hang fresh game. Her face flickered in the firelight as her eyes turned dull from horror.

"You go," said Running Moon, shoving Alvin into the gauntlet.

The little man looked around helplessly, his eyes wide with fear. "No," he whimpered.

"Run fast," advised Slocum.

Alvin hesitated. Running Moon touched the tip of his blade to one of the white man's buttocks and pushed. Loving screamed, ran into the gauntlet. Braves struck at him with sticks and fists, kicked him. He fell down several times, rose with bloodied head, his screams of terror a sickening sound above the murmuring disapproval of the Sioux.

Some of the braves began to beat the drums. Slocum looked around him at the frenzied Indians. They smelled blood now.

Running Moon looked at Slocum. "Braves heap mad," he said. "Want man, not woman."

Slocum knew what he meant. Alvin had made it through the gauntlet and was led, sobbing, back to the starting point. The two braves hurled Loving to the ground. Alvin curled up for protection, but none struck him.

They sent Raymond through next. He took it like a man. He trotted slowly, held his arms up to ward off the blows. Slocum saw him go down, then rise up, his lips smashed, one eye nearly closed, blood streaming down his cheek. He heard the sound of sticks smacking into flesh, the deep thud of moccasins landing on legs and buttocks.

The Sioux shoved Dion through the corridor of braves next. He ran fast, hunched low, missing many blows. He dodged and darted, avoiding the worst of it. The Indians cheered as he made it through with only a few cuts and bruises on him as evidence of his ordeal.

Tall Bear emerged out of the darkness and approached Slocum. He took back his shirt, then stripped the white man to the waist. The Indians brandished their warclubs and sticks.

Slocum felt the prod of Running Moon's knife in his back. He looked at Pearl for a brief moment. Her mouth was opened slightly, her breasts heaving under the bodice of her torn dress.

"White man run," said Tall Bear.

Slocum flashed a wry smile. So, the Indian had known English all along.

He started his run without any further prodding. He took long strides, raced toward the opening of the gauntlet, his arms held face-high, fists doubled.

Around him the flames of the fire grew higher, the bass throbbing of the drums even deeper.

Slocum let out a war cry of his own and crashed into the first brave who blocked his way, drove him to his knees with a short chop of his fist. He spun and whirled through the line like a dervish, his fists flailing. Sticks and clubs slammed into his rib cage; a man kneed him in the calf; another drove a fist into his kidney. He felt his knees buckle. He started to go down. Somewhere behind him he heard Raymond cheering him on. Slocum recovered and staggered on as blows rained down on his head and shoulders. He struck back, struggled forward as the Indians, furious that he was striking back, closed ranks and clogged the passageway. He drove through them and over them, knocking down a phalanx of braves who were blocking his way. He kneed, kicked, slugged, leaped over falling bodies, until he saw the last few men lining the gauntlet. His breath burned in his chest, but he drew deep down inside himself for that extra effort needed to pass through the lines.

His head rocked with a glancing blow from a warclub. A cut opened up on his forehead as something hard slashed across his eyebrows. His legs pumped faster and faster. A brave stepped out in front of him to cut him off. Slocum churned right through him, swinging a roundhouse right that knocked the brave senseless as he passed.

He was through it, panting, and his side ached, his breath tore holes in his lungs. But he was through it, and he stood there, his hands on his hips, staring at them through the blood dripping from his eyebrows, and glared at them like some regal wounded beast.

The shouting stopped. The drums went silent.

For a long moment he stood there, waiting. He thought for a moment that they were going to rush him and tear him to pieces.

Then, as if at a single silent signal, the Sioux raised their arms to the sky and shouted in praise of his courage.

"*Aaaieeeeeeee!*"

He stalked slowly back to where the others stood, passing the braves who shrank away from him as if he were a god.

"You did it, mister," said Dion, his tone laden with awe. "You got their respect."

"Mighty proud of you, sir," said Raymond.

Alvin whimpered something that Slocum couldn't hear.

Slocum looked at him. The man was in bad shape. Loving stood there bent over slightly, blood soaking through his trousers. One of his arms was broken and hung at a crazy angle. His face was purple with bruises, misshappen with ugly lumps. His breath came hard, and Slocum figured he had some ribs broken. What was it they said? A coward died a thousand deaths, but a brave man died but once.

The Indians came for them, then, lashed their wrists with thongs, shoved them rudely toward Running Moon's teepee.

The last Slocum saw of Pearl she was being stripped naked by half a dozen braves. She looked at him, her eyes pleading, but Slocum was powerless to help. He heard her scream but once before the Indians swarmed over her.

He recognized the sobs as coming from Alvin Loving.

The Professor, Raymond, Loving, and Slocum were alone in the teepee.

Slocum felt his own pain now that the worst was over. They had gotten him good. But nothing was broken. Nothing hurt that would not heal.

In the darkness, he listened to the others. They groaned and cursed from the severity of their wounds.

The teepee stank of hide and sweat and blood.

Slocum, his back seemingly on fire, tried to raise himself from his prone position.

He groaned with a pain of his own.

In the shadows he could see that Professor Dion was already sitting up.

The old man was far more frail than Slocum would have imagined. He wondered how Dion had known how to survive the gauntlet. Had he seen this before?

"What do you figure they'll do with us?"

The Professor smiled bitterly. "You're being naive, Slocum. That surprises me."

"I know they plan to kill us. I wonder what else they've got in mind."

"Well, whatever it is, they have to move quickly." There was pain in the Professor's voice. He spoke slowly and with some difficulty.

"Why?"

"I've been listening to the talk. From what I can gather, Red Cloud was sighted less than an hour ago." He shrugged pale, knobby shoulders. "Running Moon lives in dread of Red Cloud."

"You seem to know a hell of a lot about the Sioux."

"Some. There's more."

"What's that?" asked Slocum.

"Soldiers are coming. Fast. Scouts have been coming and going all night."

"You know . . ." Slocum started to say.

Alvin Loving cried out again.

Slocum went over to him. He could see now why the small man was bleeding so badly. One of the Indians had shoved a knife into his side. Slocum felt the wound. His fingers came away sticky.

"Jesus, Loving, why didn't you say something?"

Alvin moaned in pain.

For the next few minutes Slocum did what he could with the wound. With his hands bound, he could not do much. He stuffed part of Alvin's shirt in the wound. He could do nothing about the broken arm. But something inside of Loving was broken. They had done something to his insides.

"I'm dying, aren't I?" Loving said.

"No."

"Please don't lie to me."

"All right. You're dying."

A whimper again. "I wanted to prove that I was brave."

"You did prove it."

"Really?"

"Really."

"All my life I was the kind of man other men laugh at."

"Most men are stupid. Their opinions serve themselves, not the truth."

"Slocum," he said, "I'm scared."

He started to cry.

The Professor came over, and then Raymond. Loving's misery seemed to fill the lodge.

They watched him die, helplessly.

"You believe in an afterlife, Slocum?" Alvin's voice was scratchy, no more than a rasping whisper.

"I'm not sure."

"I do."

"Then there'll be one for you, I'm sure," Slocum said.

Rage was boiling up in him. He wanted to be out of this. He wanted vengeance.

"Oh, Christ, oh, dear Christ," Alvin Loving said, his pain becoming unendurable. "Will you help me, Slocum?"

"Let it take its time."

"But it hurts so much. Help me. Please."

Slocum looked over at Raymond and the Professor. The two men stared down at Alvin Loving and then they raised their heads to Slocum.

And nodded.

Slocum did it fast.

He held his hand tight over Alvin Loving's mouth and nose.

Loving writhed beneath him like a crazed beast. But not for long.

An hour or so later the camp went totally silent.

"What's going on?" Slocum whispered.

"I don't know," said Dion. "Get some sleep. They might not kill us."

"Why not?"

"If the soldiers come . . ."

Slocum listened in the darkness. He heard Dion and the black man drop off to sleep. Their breathing patterns changed.

Slocum was too angry to sleep. Sometimes there was so much to be angry at that the mind couldn't deal with it all.

He still wondered who had set him up as the one who had killed Jenks.

He still wondered who had tried to kill him, back at

the camp outside Fort Reno.

And he still wondered why Captain Scott had changed his mind and let him go after all his protests about staying off the Bozeman Trail.

The last few days of Slocum's life had reconfirmed his belief that there was no animal so treacherous as the human being.

Somehow he managed to doze off, finally, his pain a sedative.

The Indian had three fierce stripes of yellow on his chest and the same configurations, only done in blue, on his cheeks.

The warrior was the first thing Slocum saw when he came to.

The man was standing over Professor Dion and ripping out the Professor's pockets.

Before Slocum could get up to help—his bruised muscles having stiffened up during the night—he saw the man take a small leather case from Dion's pocket and examine it.

The warrior threw the flap back on the case. Inside shone a three-pointed badge.

The Indian shoved the badge at Professor Dion's face, snarling and cursing in Lakota at the old man.

Then the Indian threw back the flap of the teepee and stormed away.

For a time Slocum, Raymond, and the Professor sat in the gray light of early morning, saying nothing.

Once in a while one of them would glance over at Alvin Loving's corpse in the corner of the big tent. On the other side of the hide they could hear rats chitter hungrily.

Slocum started to say something to the Professor, but

the old man raised his hand.

"I'll save you some time, Slocum, and just tell you straight out who I am."

"Been a long time coming, Professor."

"First of all," Dion said, "I'm not a medicine drummer. I'm a military officer serving with Colonel Carrington at Fort Kearny. I'm retired, and few of the younger officers know who I am, which makes me perfect for my job."

"Which is?"

"To find out who is helping Running Moon overrun wagon trains between Fort Reno and here. At first Colonel Carrington was convinced that a white man named Calvin Jenks was responsible. Jenks stayed around Fort Reno, made friends with the people in the wagon trains there, and many times showed up in Virginia City later on with either livestock or valuables that had belonged to the people on the wagon train—who were conveniently killed by Running Moon's braves.

"Despite his reputation, Colonel Carrington is a fair man and wants to see justice done. That's why he asked me to play the Professor and travel between here and Fort Reno and see what I could find out." He shook his head. "Well, what I found out, I'm afraid, is going to make the colonel very unhappy."

"What did you find out?"

"That one of the colonel's most trusted aides works in conjunction with Calvin Jenks. I should have known from the beginning that Jenks wasn't smart enough to act alone."

Before Dion could say anything further, the flap was thrown back and a white man in a blue uniform with yellow stripes down the legs and a yellow kerchief at his neck stood smiling unpleasantly at the three men.

"I've been listening to what you were saying, Dion. A very interesting tale. Too bad Colonel Carrington will never hear it."

With that, Captain Scott took his Colt from his holster and stepped inside the teepee.

13

"Running Moon knows how to deal with prisoners," said Scott. "He is not a gentle man, I'm afraid."

The captain turned his attention to Professor Dion.

"And how is our good friend, the colonel?" Captain Scott asked.

The Professor only frowned. "You don't seem to give much of a damn about all the damage you're doing to both sides in this war, do you?"

"What I care about, to be frank," Scott said, "is more along the lines of the damage you've done me."

"A lot of white folk died because of you. So did a lot of red people."

Scott smiled over to Slocum. "Well, those things happen in war, don't they, Slocum?"

Slocum said nothing.

Raymond said, "You killed my wife by helping Running Moon."

"Where I come from, niggers don't usually speak to their superiors without being asked to speak."

Slocum shot Raymond a look and shook his head.

There was no point to be made here just yet. Scott had blood in his eye, and a pistol—a dangerous combination.

Scott's glance swept the lodge as if he was looking for trouble. He paid little attention to Loving's corpse, but his gaze lingered on Slocum. Then he reached down, grabbed Dion under the armpit, and drew the man to his feet.

"You come with me," he said tautly.

Dion looked at Slocum one last time.

Slocum dipped his head in reply.

"Gentlemen," said Dion, "I'll be seeing you, by and by."

Raymond and Slocum exchanged glances.

"I reckon," said John. "You ride easy, Dion."

Raymond, too choked up to speak, closed his eyes.

Scott shoved Dion from the teepee. A few moments later, two braves came inside. Each grabbed one of Loving's ankles, and they pulled him from the lodge.

"What do you think will happen to the Professor?" asked Raymond.

Slocum was about to reply when a pistol report broke the silence outside. The sound seemed to linger for a long time. The explosion reverberated through the hills with a kind of empty finality. Finally, even the echoes faded away.

"Lord, what kind of man is that?" Raymond said.

Slocum struggled with his bonds. The pistol shot was still ringing in his ears.

The military man returned, and poked his head inside the teepee. "I want you to suffer a little more," Captain Scott said to Slocum and Raymond. "I'll be back for you two later."

As quickly as he had said it, he was gone.

Raymond said, "I don't care what he does to me, long as I get thirty seconds at that son of a bitch."

Slocum's brows knotted up. "Move close, see if we can't untie each other," he said. "Scoot on over here."

Raymond grinned wide.

A few moments later, their hopes were dashed when a lone brave entered the teepee. He kicked the two men in the face and jerked Raymond away from John. He left them, but they heard him outside the lodge. Every few moments the brave looked in on them. Slocum continued to struggle with the thongs that bound his wrists. Later that afternoon, two guards relieved the first. Neither man saw Scott, nor did they know the fate of Pearl.

When the drums started shortly after dusk that night, Slocum peeked out the flap of the teepee to make sure that the two Indian guards were stilll there.

They were.

Each man held a Sharps carbine.

Slocum crawled back inside, his body wracked with pain. He shook his head. The more he struggled with his bonds, the tighter they cut into his flesh.

Raymond shook his head, too. "Sure hope Loving was right."

"How's that?"

"That there's a world beyond. After death, you understand?"

"Yeah."

"Because if'n there ain't, then all we are is food for the maggots."

Slocum let out a breath.

Imprisonment was starting to get Raymond. Slocum had seen this happen to men before. Their captors didn't have to worry about them. Once depression set in, the prisoners took care of themselves. Slocum had even watched men kill themselves in horrible ways.

Above the beat of the drums came a scream that could belong to nobody but Pearl.

Slocum shivered with a sudden chill. His gut was empty, but his head was clear. Where was Red Cloud? Was Scott still there? What in hell was going on?

Captain Scott lay next to the captive white woman. His eyes glittered with lust.

Running Moon had posted guards outside this teepee with instructions to let the captain alone, no matter how often or how shrilly the woman screamed.

Captain Scott tried to make Pearl compliant, tried to forget the story that Running Moon had told him about her. Last night, when some of the Indians had been about to rape her, she had gone berserk in such a way that they had thought her rabid. Even when she was lashed to the stake she fought her would-be rapists with such ferocity that, instead of making them more lustful, she frightened them instead.

One by one, the braves began to wonder if she were not an evil spirit.

Under the constant punishment of her screaming, their interest disappeared and they skulked away, leaving her untouched.

They believed that she was a crazy woman and would have nothing to do with her.

Scott knew better. She was a woman prime and in season.

He stripped off his trousers and lay against her. She was bound feet and ankles and every time she moved in protest, he grew more determined. Pearl was a prize, and you didn't find prizes very often out here on the frontier.

"Please don't," she whimpered. "You're hurting me. I don't want you."

He slapped her hard, and she screamed again. He continued rubbing against her, roiling his senses to a furious lust. Then he would stop, only making his frenzy deliciously greater. Finally, he could take it no more. He forced himself on her.

At the same time, he started hitting her, harder and harder, until he could feel bones breaking beneath his thunderous fists. Just about the time he started to come, he heard the first volleys of gunfire crackle across the sky.

Almost instantly the shouts of wounded and dying braves filled the air. Then he heard the sound of many ponies pounding into the camp.

Captain Scott did not have to wonder who was attacking.

Red Cloud had found Running Moon.

The first arrow shot through the teepee where Slocum and Raymond were being kept prisoner only moments before the second and the third arrows ripped through the buffalo hide. Each arrow was burning. The teepee was partially enflamed before the two men began to assess their predicament.

"We're either going to die here," Slocum said, "or this is a lucky break."

"I don't give a damn what happens as long as I get a chance at Captain Scott," Raymond responded.

Slocum nodded. He crawled to the tent flap and peered outside.

The camp was in utter chaos. Slocum was sure that many of the Indians in Running Moon's band were already fleeing. In the dark, it was impossible to tell who was winning. He could remember many similar scenes from his war experiences.

One brave put a tomahawk clean into the forehead of another. Then he lifted the man and threw him into the fire. The screams of dying men reached Slocum's ears.

One of the guards lay dead just outside. The other brave was gone. Slocum crawled to the dead man and pulled his knife free. Then he crawled backwards into the teepee.

"Hurry," he told Raymond. "Cut my bonds with this knife. I'll cut yours."

Raymond sawed away at the leather binding Slocum's wrists. Finally the thongs parted. Quickly, Slocum slashed Raymond's thongs. The two men looked at each other.

"Now what?" asked Raymond.

"We get the hell out of here. There's a Sharps carbine on the ground outside, and we ought to find more. I counted at least four dead."

John crept out of the tent, knife in hand.

Slocum barely saw the brave leaping at him. The warrior had Slocum's head in a vise lock in seconds.

Though slight, the man had a grip that seemed unbreakable.

He jerked Slocum away from the tent and grabbed a handful of hair.

John twisted under the warrior, shoved his knife into the Indian's soft belly. The Indian threw up his hands, dropping his own blade, and collapsed, quivering on top of Slocum.

Raymond jerked the dying brave off Slocum's chest and hurled him savagely to the ground. He kicked downward. His boot crunched into the Indian's throat, breaking his windpipe, snapping his spine.

The Indian convulsed, then was still.

Nodding to Raymond, Slocum ripped the dead warrior's knife from his hand and grabbed a Sharps from the ground in front of him. He tossed the rifle to Raymond. "Be ready to use it," he said.

"What are you going to do?"

"Find a mate to that and get some horses."

"You want me to come with you?"

"Just watch me, Raymond. You see anything come after me, shoot it."

"Yes, sir," grinned the black man.

Red Cloud's warriors streamed through the camp on painted ponies, shooting, firing the teepees. Everywhere Slocum looked, Indians were shooting Indians. Beyond the glow of burning lodges was more gunfire, savage yells, hoarse shouts. He crawled across a dead Sioux, still warm, and found a Sharps carbine, the barrel cold, unfired. He wrenched a pouch full of brass cartridges from the dead warrior's belt and checked the action. He reloaded, crawled toward a teepee. He motioned for Raymond to follow him.

Two Indians knelt in the shadows of the teepee, firing at the shadowy figures of the expert horsemen. Slocum drew a bead on one and fired from the prone position. The Indian toppled over, dead.

The other brave turned and stood up.

Tall Bear's silhouette filled Slocum's front sight. He jacked the breech open, rammed another shell into the Sharps chamber, closed the action. Tall Bear fired point-blank.

The bullet kicked up a spout of dust two yards in front of Slocum. He heard the ball whine off into the night. He rose to his feet, charged. Tall Bear, caught by sur-

prise, backed up. Slocum hit him like a battering ram,
bowling him over. He rammed the butt of the Sharps into
Tall Bear's solar plexus. A rush of air hissed through the
Indian's teeth. Slocum fell on him, straddling him in a
kneeling position. He brought the muzzle up to Tall Bear's
throat and shoved it into the soft flesh just below his
Adam's apple.

"Where's the white girl?" Slocum rasped, his anger
a terrible raging fire in his heart.

"White Eyes captain, he take white girl."

"Where?"

"White man town in mountains."

"Virginia City?"

"That place," said Tall Bear, wrenching his body upward to unseat Slocum.

John's finger touched the trigger. The explosion kicked
through the Indian's lower jaw. The ball blew his brains
out.

Raymond stopped dead in his tracks. "Jesus," he murmured.

Slocum stood up, staggered into the teepee. He had
to make sure. There was no one inside, but he smelled
the musk, saw the tangled buffalo robes. This was where
they had been. Somehow, Scott had managed to escape.
And he had taken Pearl with him. But why?

He went back outside, the weakness in him consumed
by the hatred he felt for a soldier who would betray his
own kind for the sake of a few dollars.

Slocum stripped Tall Bear's body of his own pistol
and gunbelt. He got what ammunition he could and his
own shirt. Raymond looked closely at the first Indian
Slocum had shot.

"Looks like you got Running Moon too," said Raymond. "Good shot."

The sounds of fighting faded away. Red Cloud's braves had swept through the camp like an avenging storm. Raymond and Slocum found their horses hobbled in the trees. They also found the body of Dion, lying face down next to a fir tree. He had been executed, shot in the back of the head.

They found their saddles, blankets, and bedrolls cached under a cedar. Slocum's rifle was missing, but his scabbard was still there. Gone too was Raymond's scattergun. They saddled up and rode through the trees, away from the camp.

"Where are we going?" asked Raymond when they stopped to look down at the remains of Running Moon's camp.

"See if we can't pick up Scott's trail. No use going back now. Either that wagon train makes it through or it doesn't. They'll get no help from the army."

"Captain Scott, he took the girl, huh?"

"It looks that way."

"How come? She'd just slow him down."

"Maybe he'll lay claim to rescuing her," said Slocum. "That way he's in the clear if we call him on it."

"You aim to face up to the army, Slocum?"

"Scott's not the army, Raymond. He's probably something worse."

"What's that?"

"A traitor."

Slocum picked up the tracks of the shod horse and the Indian pony just after dawn. He had set his course by the stars, circled wide, and dropped down to the Bozeman Trail a few miles south of Fort Phil Kearny.

The north fork of Clear Creek ran just south of the fort. Slocum and the black man approached the fort warily. It was quiet, just an hour shy of noon, when they rode into the empty parade ground. This was where the tracks had led them. The marks of the shod horse had continued on, but the pony's tracks showed him that it was still there.

The men rode in with cocked rifles. The pinto whickered, shook its head, pawed the ground.

"Nothin' here but ghosts," whispered Raymond.

"Maybe."

Slocum rode over to the pony. It shied away from him.

"Awful spooky," said Raymond.

"Shh. Listen."

Behind a door in what was once the sutler's store, Slocum heard a sound.

"Cover me," he said, dismounting. Raymond looked around, his eyes showing more white than brown.

Slocum rushed the door.

Raymond held his breath as the white man disappeared inside the empty store.

"God damn!" Slocum cried from inside.

"What is it?" Raymond asked quickly, his voice trembling with a nameless fear.

"It's Pearl," said Slocum, his voice hollow, eerie in the emptiness of the room.

"What about her?" Raymond said.

Slocum said, "She's here."

"So?"

"She's dead."

The black man tied the horses to the hitchrail and dashed inside.

Pearl lay in a corner, her eyes closed. She didn't seem to be breathing. Slocum laid his rifle down.

"We got a mirror?" asked Raymond.

Slocum broke out a windowpane. He handed a sliver to the black man.

Raymond's mama had taught him the mirror trick. He held the fragment of glass under Pearl's nose until finally a tiny bit of mist appeared on the surface.

Slocum sighed loudly.

"Damn," he said.

He said it like a prayer of thanks.

By early afternoon they had her sitting up and huddled inside a blanket. At first she didn't quite seem to know who they were or why they were there. But gradually she began to remember things, and when she recalled exactly who she was and exactly what had happened she began to weep.

Slocum let her cry. Raymond kept watching the door, looking out through the broken window. It was quiet, and he was nervous.

"Is that woman ever going to stop crying?" he blurted in desperation.

Slocum knelt beside her. "Pearl. It's all right. We're going to take care of you." He put a hand on her shoulder.

She cringed, then stared at him. Something like recognition dawned in her eyes. She opened her mouth to speak. Nothing came out.

Then she said, "He went on to Virginia City."

"Scott?"

"Yes."

"We know that," said Slocum.

"I want to—to go there," she said.

"Why?"

"To kill him." She shuddered.

"No," Slocum said. "That's my job."

14

Slocum didn't know it, but his wagon train was the last to use the Bozeman Trail. There would never be a book on it, because there was no one at the forts to record its passing. He, Raymond, and Pearl holed up in abandoned Fort Phil Kearny while the Sioux swept the south trail clean, and before they got around to burning it to the ground. The hated Fort C. F. Smith, that lonesome outpost, was already burned by the time Slocum and his two companions reached it a month later. The adobe walls were still standing, their walls blackened with soot, mute testimony to the hatred the Sioux carried for the whites who traveled through their lands.

Slocum and the others healed, lived off wild game, herbs, roots, and berries, for the autumn lingered on until the aspen's yellow leaves fell, and the once-bright leaves of the hardwoods turned rust before they too dropped to the ground and rattled along the game trails like skeletons when the fall breezes turned brisk. Slocum grew hard again, strong. Pearl drifted in and out of a kind of insanity, making sense only in lucid moments. Raymond brooded, fished the streams for trout using flint hooks he found and worms dug from the soft banks after rain.

They rode past Fort Smith, listening for its ghosts, looking at the shadows dripping from the burned wall like the cast-off uniforms of a retreating army. Cattle tracks frozen in mud told Slocum that his herd had passed by some time ago and he had never known it because they had avoided Fort Kearny, and the Sioux as well. Late in the afternoon, when the shadows lay strewn across the empty trail, Slocum halted his horse and listened. It seemed he had heard a bugle call in the distance, back where the fort lay in ruins, but it was only a trick of the wind.

The deer were plentiful, and they ate well. The horses grew lean on the sparse grasses, but their pace was slow. Pearl often sang to herself during the day, her eyes glassy and empty like the eyes of fish lying dead and metallic-looking on a creek bank. In the evenings, she often smiled at Slocum and Raymond, and thanked them for being so kind to her. Then she would shiver and turn away and the men would hear her weeping to herself like a broken-hearted child.

They rode into a post cemetery by accident one day, and Raymond could not stand to be there. Pearl looked longingly at the graves, and her eyes went wet for no reason that Slocum could tell. When they rode away, she kept looking back like a child going away from home for the first time.

"Who are they?" she asked.

"People. Families. Soldiers. Travelers."

"Where did Raymond go?"

"He doesn't like graveyards."

"They're quiet. So peaceful," she said.

"Come on," he gruffed, wondering at himself, wondering why he could not look into Pearl's haunted eyes just then.

They moved slowly through the agonizing days of autumn and tasted snow on the air, and felt the chill in their bones when they rose at dawn. Once they saw a small band of Sioux who looked at them and perhaps remembered the crazy woman with the hair like wheat, like the faded aspen leaves, and left them alone, rode on into the hills as if they had always owned them, always would.

Slocum did not get closer to Pearl, and Raymond could not talk to her for very long without getting depressed.

"I think of my wife," he told Slocum one day, "and I thank God she died instead of being captured and raped."

"Don't think about it," Slocum said.

"I think about it, mister, and I think about that white trash Scott, and I get to boiling inside until I can hardly stand it."

"Yeah. Well, I think about Scott too, and those Texans, Rossiter and Shoop."

"Think they sold off your cattle."

"They or Scott. Same difference."

They talked of these things some, and when they rode into Virginia City just ahead of winter, the men were bitter with their thoughts and Pearl was vacant-eyed as a doll, her blond hair faded and clogged with burrs because she no longer cared about herself, her skin dull with dirt because she would not bathe since she had seen the post graveyard and something in herself that was dead or dying.

There had been rain. The streets were muddy, with men driving mules through knee-deep slush, cursing, spitting tobacco juice. The saloons were raucous, the clatter inside competing with the throng of grimy men and loose women streaming past outside like homeless immigrants.

Slocum, the ex-slave, and Pearl walked the planks that spanned the sea of mud in the streets, looking in store windows, reading the signs that proclaimed the cost of goods.

"Man can't live here without money," said Raymond. "I ain't got a single dime."

"I've got a few dollars tucked in my boot. We'll get a hotel, bathe, and buy some clothes."

"You'd stake me?"

"A gift," said Slocum.

"Charity, you mean."

"No, Raymond, I don't mean that at all. Call it a salary if you want. I've hired you to help me get either my cattle back or the price paid for them."

"Seeing how you put it that way, Mr. Slocum, I'd be right proud to have a coin or two in my empty pocket." He grinned wide and sidestepped a grizzled miner who was staggering by, three sheets to the wind.

Ore wagons and stagecoaches jammed the streets. Gunfire crackled at least once every twenty minutes. The occasional respectable woman or pilgrim looked confused by the sights and sounds around them, as if they could not understand how humankind could sink as low as it had here in Virginia City.

They found a hotel that looked cheap enough, with rooms to let. Slocum took a double room, slipped off his boot, took out a wad of bills. The clerk asked no questions, but counted the sweat-soaked money twice. Upstairs, Slocum saw Pearl to her adjoining room and spoke to her.

"I'm going to try and find your ... ah ... sisters," he said. "Will you stay here until I get back?"

"I'm afraid." Her voice trembled.

"Better you stay here. The door will be locked. Are you hungry?"

She shook her head and walked to the window. She looked down, turned away, sat on the bed. She folded her hands in her lap.

"I'll buy you a dress, Pearl." Slocum bit back his bitterness. He saw that there was a basin, water in the pitcher. He closed the door between the rooms.

Raymond looked at himself in a cracked mirror hanging from the wall over the highboy. He rubbed the thick beard on his face. "Ain't I a sight?"

Slocum did not recognize himself. His beard was thick and scraggly. He cracked a smile.

"Let's get some duds, a shave, and find a bathhouse," he said. "I want to buy Pearl a dress."

"You got that much money?"

"Burying money and then some."

Slocum and Raymond went to look up any cattle buyers they could find for some lead to Slocum's five hundred head. Clean-shaven, bathed, dressed in new clothes, the two men went from broker to broker, trying to get a lead on Slocum's cattle. All but one said they were too busy to answer a lot of questions. The last man they saw, though curt, was more helpful.

"Was a big herd come up the Bozeman 'bout a week ago," he said. "Pretty decent stock. Went for twenty-five a head."

"Know where I can find the men who drove them up?" asked Slocum.

"Try the saloons. You're looking for a couple of

Texans and a captain."

"Much obliged," said Slocum, stifling a grin.

Over beers and shots in the first saloon, Raymond said, "Looks like Scott and those Texans stole your herd."

"I reckon so. Maybe that's to our advantage."

"How come?"

"Don't worry," Slocum said.

His idea was simple enough. He planned to use his herd as evidence of Scott's complicity with Running Moon. He would take that evidence to Colonel Carrington. Pearl, if she was rational enough, could testify that she saw Scott with Running Moon's band.

A lilting fragrance of a gentle perfume brushed his nostrils. Slocum turned to find Emily Schoolcraft standing behind him.

Both Raymond and Slocum stared at the woman with disbelieving eyes. Gone was the proper, Bible-toting woman. In her stead was a beautiful, bosomy, but painted-up whore. A Virginia City vixen, to be sure.

Only her eyes betrayed her real feelings. She did not look happy there in her silk dress with her breasts spilling out so that the dark aureoles showed.

Behind her a number of grimy sourdoughs pawed the air she had just passed through and made loud and primitive gestures and suggestions. She didn't seem to notice them.

"What're you doing here?" Slocum asked edgily.

"Working," she said.

"I can see that."

"I take it you don't approve."

"It's a little late to ask for my opinion."

She smiled. "You're jealous, aren't you?"

"I don't know," he admitted.

"At least you're honest about it."

"We found Pearl," he said.

"Is —is she . . ."

"She'll live, if she's got the will. They worked her over pretty good. The Sioux and that bastard Scott."

Tears flushed her eyes. She tried to hold them back. Raymond looked away, swallowed whiskey. Slocum let her fall into his arms. Her tears came more freely now. She started to sob.

Slocum took her arm gently and guided her through the mob of miners. He found a back room used for storage. He led her inside and kicked the door shut with his boot heel.

Early afternoon sunlight fell in a thin golden bar on the hardwood floor.

"Captain Scott must have been unbelievable to her," Emily said, after listening to Slocum's story. "You say she's in a trance?" Emily started sobbing again.

"Something like that. Like the heart's gone out of her."

"Those beasts. And Captain Scott . . . it's hard to believe."

"Believe it. Maybe you can tell me what you know."

After Slocum and Raymond and Alvin Loving had left the wagon train, Rossiter took over as boss of the wagon train, with Shoop siding him, Lee Dimmock throwing in with both of them. One night Captain Scott showed up and it was obvious that Rossiter and he had struck some kind of bargain. Captain Scott and his handful of troops rode out of camp. Presumably this was when they had met up with Running Moon and Slocum.

Rossiter and Shoop drove Slocum's herd on into Virginia City and sold it with a forged bill of sale for a good price.

"How the hell do you know all this?" Slocum asked.

He sneezed right after he spoke. The storage room held big sacks of grain and dried hops.

"Lee Dimmock told me."

"Dimmock? Why would he cooperate? I thought he was with Rossiter and Shoop."

"He's also, I'm ashamed to say, my ex-husband."

Slocum's jaw went slack with surprise. "Lee Dimmock?"

Emily explained that she'd married Dimmock when she'd still had hopes of being a normal human being. He hadn't exactly helped her plans along, encouraging her to be a whore so that he could enjoy the fruits of her labor.

"He *wanted* you to sleep with other men?"

Emily nodded, looking as if she didn't know whether to laugh or cry. "It's funny, isn't it? I couldn't tell you what I saw in the man, why I loved him so much, or why I let him treat me that way. Lee just figured it was easier to let me be a whore than to find a job for himself. When I finally got sense enough to break off with him, I saw that he still couldn't take care of himself, so I kept him on as a kind of all-purpose handyman and driver. He got into trouble from time to time—he's always looking for the big opportunity—but until now he's never thrown in with people like Rossiter and Shoop and Captain Scott." She shook her head and started crying again. "Especially Captain Scott. John, he can't get away with this. I hope you really are going to kill him."

"I should, but if Carrington will listen to me . . ."

"He won't. Scott bragged about that."

"Is he still here? In Virginia City?"

"Yes."

Emily slid into Slocum's arms. "Just because I went back to my old ways doesn't mean that I don't believe the truth of the Bible and everything I said to you."

"I know."

"I'm only doing it so I can raise enough money to go into a legitimate business."

Slocum sighed. "You don't owe me any explanations."

"For some reason, I feel like I do."

"Do you want to see Pearl? She's at the Alder. I rented a couple of rooms. Ten and twelve."

"I—I know it. I'll see her when . . . after work."

"Yeah," said Slocum. She reached for him, but he stepped away.

"Where are you going?"

"To find Rossiter and Shoop," he said.

Before she could reply, he was gone.

Around dusk, and a chill dusk it was, the whores all wearing shawls and their customers huddled inside buffalo coats and sheepskin jackets, Slocum and Raymond found out where Rossiter and Shoop were staying.

On the side of a clapboard barbershop a flight of stairs teetered up to a second-floor loft that rented out as a domicile.

Several drunks in the High Times saloon had informed Slocum and Raymond that this was where they were likely to find the two men.

"Up over Shorty's tonsorial parlor."

Slocum and Raymond stood in the shadowy quiet of the dying day, checking their weapons, keeping a furtive eye out for anybody paying them undue attention. There was no lamp burning in the second-story flat.

"Think they're up there?" asked Raymond.

"We've hit every saloon in town. If they aren't here, they're not in town."

"What if they're waiting for us?"

"They could be," said Slocum. "We get up there, you wait outside while I go in."

Raymond swore. He hefted the Spencer. It wouldn't be any good at close quarters, anyway.

Slocum led out and climbed the stairs slowly. Behind him, Raymond stepped when he did. The rickety stairs creaked. Slocum drew his pistol, kept his eyes fixed on the door. If it opened, he was ready.

The door didn't open.

They made the landing. Raymond hugged the wall. Slocum knocked on the door. There was no reply.

He looked at Raymond and shrugged. Raymond's eyebrows lifted.

"I'm going in," said Slocum. "If they open up, or if I don't come out, you lay into them."

Raymond nodded.

Slocum lifted the latch. It came free. The door swung open. He stood to one side and peered through the gloom.

"Christ," he whispered.

Rossiter and Shoop lay sprawled on the floor in the center of the room. They were dead. Pools of blood stood glistening on the bare wood. Two puddles.

Slocum stepped inside and looked at the bodies closely. Each of them had been shot cleanly, execution-style, through the back of the head.

The sleeping room was not much bigger than the birthing area in a barn. Two bedrolls had been laid out on either side of a big kerosene lamp. A tin pan rank with piss stood in a corner.

Raymond entered the room, blinking to adjust his focus. "They're dead as doornails," he said.

"Yeah. See anything familiar about how they died?"

Raymond forced himself to look. Vacant eyes gazed

out of the sockets of the two men. Shoop had tried to draw his pistol. It lay half out of its holster, his fingers locked around the butt in a death grip. Rossiter had evidently been shot first. Both men had their shirttails out, their pockets turned inside out. Empty saddlebags lay against the wall where someone had hurled them. The room too had been gone over, searched.

"Like Professor Dion," said the black man.

"Exactly." Slocum turned, finished with his examination of the room.

Then they heard the noise on the steps outside.

Slocum put a finger to his lips.

He crossed on tiptoe to the door in seconds, his gun ready.

One, two, three tentative footsteps sounded on the stairs outside.

They stopped. Slocum stood by the door. He eased the hammer back, holding the trigger in slightly so that there was no sound.

The stairs creaked as the footsteps started up again.

A man's figure filled the doorway. Slocum rammed the pistol barrel into the man's heavy coat.

"Please, Slocum," Lee Dimmock begged. "Don't shoot me."

Slocum let out a breath.

"Step inside, Dimmock. Move slow and keep your hands where I can see them."

"I—I didn't know you were here," said Dimmock. It was obvious he was shaken; he didn't expect to see them there. He looked down at the bodies and up at Raymond. "Did you kill them?" he breathed.

"No," said Slocum. "But I'll ask the questions. What are you doing here?"

"I wanted the money."

"What money?"

"The money Captain Scott gave them."

"Their part of the cattle sale?"

"Yeah."

"How much?"

"Scott gave 'em four thousand, I think."

Raymond whistled.

"How much did they get for the cattle?" asked Slocum.

"They sold four hunnert and eight-five head. Got twenty-five apiece."

Slocum did some figuring.

"Twelve thousand and some change," he said bitterly.

"Who—who..." Dimmock looked around, saw how the room had been torn up. "Did you find the money?"

"You don't know who killed them, Dimmock?" Slocum was running out of patience.

"No. I thought you did. I mean, at first."

"Scott killed them, and then he took his money back. Now Scott's got all the money."

Dimmock's face turned pale.

Slocum said, "And you're next."

"God help me."

"I'd be willing to help you," Slocum said.

"You would?"

"Yeah. If you'd help me."

"Like what?"

"Go with me to Colonel Carrington. Tell him all about Scott."

"Damn," Dimmock said.

"If you don't, I won't help you at all," Slocum said.

"Yeah," Raymond said. "We just let Captain Scott get you in your sleep."

Dimmock's face screwed up and he began to tremble.

Slocum felt like killing him on the spot. For his part in this, for what he did to Emily, for just being a miserable bastard of a human being.

But he wouldn't kill him. Not now.

He knew what he had to do.

He had to keep Dimmock alive.

15

Slocum checked Dimmock for weapons.

"All right, you walk ahead of us," said Slocum. "We're going to see Carrington now."

"What if Scott sees us first?"

"Then he'll sweat."

Dimmock moved as Slocum prodded him. He didn't make it past the door.

A shot cracked from somewhere below. Dimmock clutched his belly, pitched backwards, gutshot.

Slocum hunched low, scrambled over the writhing man's body, his pistol leveled. He saw a uniformed figure standing by the building where he and Raymond had been moments before.

Raymond came up behind Slocum and peered over the railing.

"That's him," he said. "That's Captain Scott."

Slocum took aim.

Captain Scott rounded the corner and disappeared. Slocum and Raymond heard boots pounding on rickety boards.

"I'll catch him," said Raymond, bounding down the stairs.

"I'll be right behind you," said Slocum.

He turned to see what he could do for Dimmock. The man lay still, doubled up in pain. The shadows were thick now in the room, thick in Dimmock's eyes. It was rapidly turning dark now that the sun had set.

"Dimmock?"

A throaty sound came from the dying man's lips.

Slocum saw the wound, the smashed intestines. There was nothing he could do for the man. Probably nothing a doctor could do. The lead bullet had gone in low, ripped up into the man. Blood seeped from the corners of Dimmock's lips.

"You have any prayers, now's the time to say 'em," said Slocum.

"Ah, tell Emily..."

"Yeah?"

"Sorry..."

Dimmock shuddered. Something final, brittle, rattled in his throat. Slocum stood up and holstered his pistol. He wondered now if he could have gotten off a shot at the captain. Maybe not. There was nothing more he could do here. Maybe Raymond would catch up to Scott. That would make it simple. Except he might be tried for murder. The one good witness lay dead on the floor. Dimmock might have come through for him. Might have...

Suddenly it all seemed hopeless to Slocum. He kept reaching, grabbing, but all he came up with was sand, and even that trickled through his fingers. He didn't know if Pearl would prove to be a reliable witness. He thought of her now, and of Emily.

A sound jarred him back to the present.

A distant gunshot, muffled. Nothing unusual in Virginia City. But this one seemed so final.

He searched everywhere for signs of Raymond and Captain Scott. No one had seen anything. No one knew anything.

Slocum went back to his room. Raymond was not there. Neither was Pearl.

He pounded downstairs, woke up the night clerk.

"I'm Slocum," he said. "Did you see a blond woman go out? Wearing a new calico dress? A coat?"

"Yeah. Miz Schoolcraft come and took her. Said they was sisters."

"How about a black man? You see him?"

"No, I reckon not."

"Where does Emily Schoolcraft live?"

The clerk laughed harshly. "Hell, you don't know? Everybody else does."

Slocum reached over, grabbed the clerk by the shirtfront, jerked him half over the desk. "You want to make fun, go right to it, son. I want some straight answers from you, no smart lip."

"Damn, man, all right. Just let me go. The Schoolcraft sisters live at the end of Alder, little clapboard shack. Got red curtains in the winders."

"Alder?"

"Off of Main, two blocks. Rinker's Saloon on one corner, Dan's Butcher Shop on the other."

Slocum released the man and stalked from the hotel. Again, everything was slipping from his fingers. Emily had every right to take Pearl home with her, but the way it looked, Scott didn't want any witnesses alive to testify against him. He had killed three men this day, and he wouldn't hesitate to kill Pearl. The man was merciless, desperate.

Slocum waded through clutches of people making their way up and down the mud-clogged street, stepping on the jumble of boards that seemed to have been tossed here and there by some mad builder. Mining towns like this always attracted gamblers as well as whores, minstrels as well as peddlers, people who thrived on the night.

He found Alder Street. It was one long row of shacks, all with red lanterns dangling from the eaves.

Emily Schoolcraft's place was in the red-light district.

On his way there, Slocum passed several soldiers. He kept his hat low and his gun ready. They gave him no trouble.

The Schoolcraft house was as the desk clerk had described it. No lantern, but the drapes glowed with a warm red light.

He knocked once and fell back into the shadows.

Wearing a wrapper, Emily peeked out and jumped when Slocum whispered her name.

"Are you alone?"

"Except for Jennie and Pearl, yes."

"Can I come in?"

"Of course."

Lamplight bathed the room that was made up to resemble a parlor, with doilies over the backs of its couch and chair, with a large painting of a New England harbor on the west wall. Another, a print, depicted men in livery riding to hounds in smoky Virginia hills, a red fox just topping a rise in the background. There was a hallway, and he saw lamplight spilling from what he gathered were three small rooms. Bedrooms to most people. To Emily and the girls, working rooms as well. The room smelled faintly of whiskey and sour sweat and tobacco. The dusty scent of perfume couldn't hide it. Men had been here.

Yet the room was neat, the brass lamps polished to a high golden sheen, the floor immaculate. There was a bar, dusted bottles atop its smooth surface, a small desk in one corner, its walnut finish gleaming with rubbed-in oils, a bookcase. He walked to it, surprised, because he had seen no book besides the Bible in the Schoolcraft wagon. He glanced at the titles, all strange to him.

"You read these books?" he asked.

"Oh, those. We entertain troops stationed at the garrison. They donated those to our small library."

"Pretty heavy fare," he observed.

Emily smiled at Slocum sadly. "I'm sorry for all your trouble, John," she said, changing the subject.

"Thank you." He didn't take off his hat. He would not stay long.

"Alvin Loving is dead," he said.

"Yes."

"You knew?"

Emily's face flushed pink momentarily.

"Well, I imagined. He wasn't with you and Raymond. He was a dear little man."

"A brave one as it turns out too." Saying those words gave Slocum pleasure. He had begun to admire Alvin Loving for shorning himself of his wife and finally acting like a man. "How's Pearl?"

Emily nodded to one of the small rooms. She took Slocum's arm, pressing one of her nice breasts against it, guiding him over to where Pearl sat unmoving in a rocking chair behind a beaded curtain.

"Pearl."

Nothing.

"Pearl, John Slocum is here."

Again nothing.

Looking at her pretty features in the light of the lantern next to her, Slocum saw that Pearl did indeed seem to be in some kind of trance. She was staring straight ahead.

Slocum was familiar with the effect of terrible shock on the mind. He had seen a lot of it in the War.

"Pearl," Emily repeated.

Emily led Slocum through the beaded curtains and they knelt in front of Pearl while Emily held her hand. Slocum just watched the woman, touched by her grief and her wan prettiness, and all the more determined to finish the task at hand with Captain Scott. He looked at the bed. It was more like a large bunk. The blanket was stretched as taut as a trampoline. A coin dropped on its surface would bounce. He leaned close to Pearl, drew back when he caught a whiff of her breath.

"She smells like a distillery," he said.

"I gave her some brandy to calm her down, soothe her nerves, poor girl."

Slocum looked closely at Pearl again. It was difficult to tell if she was still touched in the head, or just plain drunk.

Emily took a Bible and put it in Pearl's lap, then took Pearl's hand and pressed it gently to the book. Emily closed her eyes and said, "Lord, grant her strength."

Slocum wondered if prayer could help. Pearl didn't seem to know anyone was in the room with her.

"Do you remember John? He's your friend," Emily said to Pearl.

For just a moment there was a flicker of recognition in Pearl's eyes. She looked over at John and a tiny smile tugged at her cupid's mouth. Then all recognition died again. Pearl's eyes went vacant, cold as stone.

Emily started weeping softly.

Slocum led her out of the room.

"We can talk now," said Emily. "Jennie? John Slocum's here. Send your friend home out the back way."

Slocum heard noises down the hall. Beyond the rooms, he saw the barest glimmer of a table, a stove in the kitchen. Lanternlight shone through a window, red as a barn. So the back porch was an entrance as well, perhaps for visitors who did not want to be seen visiting a house of ill repute.

"I told her we'd not work tonight. I do hope you don't mind my bringing Pearl here. She—she was so lost up there. We gave her some broth, bathed her."

Now Slocum knew why there was no lighted lantern on the front porch. The house was closed to customers for the evening. He gathered Emily worked the saloon during the afternoons and here in the evenings. Well, a woman had to get along as best she could. Emily was good at what she did, whether she sold it or gave it away.

"Whiskey?" Emily held up a bottle.

"Fine," he said. "You didn't see Raymond this evening, did you?"

"Why, no. Was he coming here?"

"No."

Emily's back was to him. He saw her lean over the table, heard a glass rattle, the whisper of something he couldn't define. Then she stood straight up and he heard the slosh of liquid, the gurgle from the throat of the bottle. She swirled the whiskey in the glass. Idly, he wondered why. It didn't appear to be Taos Lightning or rotgut, but clear, good whiskey. The label on the bottle said Old Overholt. Good stuff.

He heard whispers down the hall, a man's low voice, Jennie saying something urgent. He would have expected a giggle or two. He cleared his throat, feeling oddly uncomfortable. Emily moved stiffly toward him. He saw that she had poured a considerable amount of whiskey into a tall glass. He took it from her, looked up at her face. She avoided his gaze as footsteps moved down the hall.

Jennie came in and looked at Slocum without saying anything. Her hair was tousled, her wrapper half open so that he could see her breasts, the flash of her legs. She poured herself a drink, and that was when he saw the hard lines etched into her face. Her hands shook slightly until she got the drink down. She moved something under the settee. It looked, Slocum thought, like a cavalry boot. He hadn't noticed it there before.

"I need your help," said Slocum when the two women were settled down on the settee. He sat in a large easy chair, his drink in his hand.

"If it means getting Scott, I'll do anything. After what he did to Pearl . . ."

Emily shook her head. The tears came again. Jennie put her arms around Emily and held her hand.

Jennie said, "Either one of us would help you in any way you need, John."

"Good," Slocum said. "I doubt if Pearl can tell Carrington what Scott did to her. But you could testify that my cattle were stolen. If they search Scott's room, they'll find more money than he can make on a captain's pay."

"Your money?"

"Yes."

"We don't know anything about that," said Jennie. "Do we, Emily?"

The two women exchanged glances.

Slocum squirmed. What was going on here?

"I wouldn't say that, Jennie. John, she's scared," Emily went on. "So am I. Those men, Rossiter and Shoop.

They're hard men. Killers. And they're in with Captain Scott, I'm sure."

"They're dead now. Dimmock too."

Both women drew back in shock. Their faces drained of blood, turned chalk-white.

"You? Did you kill them?" asked Emily.

"No. Scott did."

Slocum waited out the silence that followed his explanation of what had happened to the three men only an hour or so before.

"We'll tell the colonel what we know," said Emily. "Won't we, Jennie dear?"

Jennie smiled crookedly, and Slocum realized how much whiskey the woman must have drunk. She looked as insane as Pearl.

Slocum knew something was wrong before he was half-finished with his whiskey. He felt light-headed and woozy. Iron bands tightened around his chest. The air in the room became suddenly warm, close, stifling. He struggled to draw in a breath. The room spun. He opened a button on his shirt. When he started to rise, to go to the front door for some fresh air, he knew his legs wouldn't make it. They were numb, lifeless as wooden sticks.

"Ah," he gasped.

Emily and Jennie rose from the settee, flanked him on the arms of the easy chair. Emily ran nervous fingers through his hair.

"What's the matter, John?" she asked. "Getting a little drunk?" Her voice sounded cottony, far away.

Jennie rubbed a hand across his chest. He felt suddenly peaceful, carefree. Emily leaned down, kissed him gently on the lips. He should have felt a surge of pleasure in his loins, an electric tingle in his spine, but he felt nothing. Nothing but a smothering sensation as it became difficult to breathe. The glass in his hand tumbled to the floor, and he realized he didn't give a damn.

Neither woman made a move to pick up the glass. He thought that was odd, too, but he couldn't focus on any of the words flitting through his mind. He saw the words, but they were formless, didn't make any sense. He felt like laughing, but there was a fog clouding his brain and he blinked his eyes, trying to clear it out.

From somewhere, beyond his mind, he heard a door slam, then the tramp of boots on hard wood. None of it made any sense to him. Emily's hand slid down his face, and then Jennie was leaning over him, pressing a breast against his face, a soft, creamy breast with the nipple brushing against his nose.

"You shouldn't have come back, John," said Emily. "It would have been better if you had gone back where you came from."

"You're not going to get the money," said Jennie. "Part of it's ours, isn't it, Emily?"

The noises got louder, and then the women drew away from him. He struggled to his feet, knowing something was wrong. He stood on wobbly legs, swayed with a drunkenness he knew, by God, he shouldn't have. The room spun and he saw the blue uniforms and the rifles. Three men, two of them standing straight as lodgepoles, came into focus in front of him. One of the men stepped forward and drew a pistol.

He vaguely recognized the face of the man with the pistol. The two men with rifles were just faceless soldiers. But the man with the pistol had gold bars on his shoulders, brass buttons on his tunic, and his lips were curled back from his teeth in a wolfish grin.

Yes, Slocum knew the man. Even in his fog-bound

stupor he knew him. He tried to move his leaden arms, untangle dead fingers. Thoughts swirled in his brain, but he couldn't sort them out, couldn't make his arms or hands or legs work. And, as surely as he knew that he was sinking into a black, bottomless pit, he knew he was going to die if he didn't climb out before it was too late.

"Strip that gunbelt from your waist, Slocum, or it will be my pleasure to kill you right now," Captain Scott said.

16

Slocum blinked and took a deep breath.

His head cleared momentarily. Captain Scott came into focus.

"What did you give him?" asked the captain.

"A powder in his drink," said Emily. "From the apothecary."

"Will it kill him?"

Emily laughed. "No, but any other man would have been sleeping like a baby. Of course, he only drank half his drink."

Scott turned his attention to Slocum again.

"I said to drop your gunbelt. You're wanted for murder, Slocum."

Slocum's hand dropped to his buckle. The feeling returned to his fingers. He worked the tongue free of the hole. His belt and holster fell away from his waist. Jennie reached down quickly, picked his rig up, and threw it on the settee. Slocum saw that she was not drunk after all. She had moved pretty fast.

"What are you going to do with him, Bill?" asked Emily.

Scott laughed harshly. "When you sent that soldier to me with the message that Slocum was here, Jennie, I immediately went to Colonel Carrington with Slocum's wagon book. Proof that he was in cahoots with Running Moon."

Still woozy, John tried to make sense of the captain's words. "I didn't have a wagon book . . ." he said.

"Keep your mouth shut," said Scott, interrupting. Then: "Corporal, arrest this man for the murders of Calvin Jenks and Brevet Major Harold Dion."

"You lyin' son of a bitch," said Slocum, fighting against the fog in his skull.

The two soldiers stepped forward, grabbed his arms. Captain Scott smiled with smug satisfaction.

"There will be other charges, I'm sure," said Scott. "As soon as Colonel Carrington reads the wagon book, I believe he'll have enough evidence to hang you a dozen times."

"A man can only die once, Scott," said Slocum, taking deep breaths to clear his head. He knew now what Emily had given him. He had heard of it during the War. Some called it "Shanghai powder," others, of Irish descent, call the chemical a "Mickey Finn." It was a tool used by unscrupulous men and whores when they wanted to roll a drunk. Emily continued to surprise him.

He hadn't known about the wagon book until now. If the Bozeman Trail had been open, he knew he would have been required to keep a log, have the book signed at each military post. But the Trail had been closed down, and no one had asked him for such a book at Fort Reno. Apparently, Scott had made one up anyway, and forged his name to it. The bastard.

The two soldiers held him tightly, awaiting further orders.

"Sir?" said one.

"I want this man taken to the garrison immediately," said Scott.

The men started to take Slocum away, when there was the sound of hoofbeats coming up the street. The women wore startled looks on their faces.

Scott frowned. "Hold up a minute," he told the troopers.

They all heard the sound of horses surrounding the house, the rattle of sabers, the slap and creak of leather. The sounds seemed to fill the room.

"What is it, Bill?" asked Emily. "Did you order your men to come here?"

"No, damn it," said Scott. "Shut up a minute. Let me think."

The colonel didn't knock on the door. He strode in, carrying a ledger in gloved hands, dressed in full military regalia. Four troopers ushered him in. One, a sergeant, carried a large sack in his hands.

"Atten-hut!" sounded the corporal next to Slocum. Scott and the other troopers drew up to attention.

The next person through the door was the ex-slave, Raymond.

Slocum felt a rush of blood to his face. He had never expected to see the black man alive again. His lips curled in a slow smile.

Colonel Henry B. Carrington, though blameless, had been accused in the popular press of being derelict in the matter of the Fetterman massacre. Indeed, ill luck had dogged his footsteps ever since Brigadier General Philip St. George Cooke had put him in command of the Second Battalion of the Eighteenth U.S. Infantry and told him to build and man three proposed forts that would keep the Bozeman Trail open. He had been ordered to dismantle Fort Reno and move it forty miles farther up the trail, but there were too many supplies there, so he left the fort where it was and built Fort Phil Kearny and Fort C.F. Smith on the Big Horn. He never did build a fort on the upper Yellowstone, because he did not have enough troops to man it. Now, in disgrace, his expedition known as "Carrington's Overland Circus," he was a dour, humorless man with a graying beard and moustache.

"Captain Scott," he said, "what is the meaning of this? Who is this civilian?"

"Sir, this is the man I told you about, the murderer, one John Slocum."

Carrington turned to Slocum. "Is this your wagon trail book, Slocum?" asked the colonel, point-blank.

"No," said Slocum, his tongue thick in his mouth.

"I thought not. Captain Scott, do you know this black man, an ex-slave who calls himself Raymond?"

"I've seen the man. He's in cahoots with—"

"When I want your opinion, I'll ask for it. Sir, you answer my questions, and speak the truth, or I'll have your hide."

"Yes, sir."

"These women? You know them?"

"Why, yes. I . . . ah . . . well, sir, they are prepared to testify against this John Slocum."

"Damn it, man, don't stutter, and don't run on so. You are away from your post without orders, without permission, in a house of ill repute, making an arrest not within your authority. Troopers, release that civilian and stand at attention."

"Yes, sir!" chorused the two men holding Slocum.

They released their grips on Slocum's arms, stepped to one side briskly, and stood straight at attention.

"Slocum, are you drunk?"

"Some. Drugged."

"Do you wish to be seated?"

"No, Colonel. I might not get up again." Slocum's speech was slurred, but he was gaining on the drug in his bloodstream.

"Very well," said the colonel, "let's get down to cases. Captain, this book is an outright travesty, a fabrication. How do you explain it, sir?"

"Colonel, I signed this book at Fort Reno, and directed this man to get off the Bozeman Trail. When he refused, I gave the book to one Calvin Jenks, who was subsequently murdered by Slocum here. Those facts in there were recorded by Rossiter and Shoop, duly witnessed by one Lee Dimmock. I'm sure these women here can testify..."

"Don't tell me what anyone can do, sir," snapped Carrington. "All of the men you mentioned are dead. This Negro here told me that you dispatched my close friend, Harold Dion, by firing a pistol ball through the back of his head. My investigation reveals that Shoop, Rossiter, and Dimmock were dispatched in the same manner."

"Sir, I know nothing about—"

"Silence! I'll conduct this investigation." The colonel tweaked his moustache, strolled in a tight circle, hands folded behind his back. He came to a halt, his face a dozen inches away from Slocum's.

"Did you murder any of those men, Slocum?"

"No, sir."

"That's what this Negro tells me. He also says that

you rescued a white woman from Running Moon's band. And that our Captain Scott here was friendly to that renegade."

"I reckon that's about it," Slocum drawled. "If my head was clearer, I could fill in some blanks."

"Yes, I'm sure. Captain Scott, are you getting my drift?"

"Sir?" Scott said tightly.

"Don't parry with me, sir," said the colonel, turning to face the captain. "Sergeant Wales!" The colonel snapped his fingers. A trooper with three chevrons on his sleeve stepped forward. He was the man with the burlap sack in his hands.

"Set that strongbox on the floor here, where Captain Scott won't fail to see it."

The sergeant opened the sack and withdrew a metal strongbox. He set it on the floor in the center of the room.

"Open it, Sergeant," said Carrington.

The trooper knelt down, rattled the lid, and opened the box.

It was filled with greenbacks.

Scott's face blanched.

"A thorough search was made of your quarters, Captain Scott, and the quartermaster counted this currency, which was found hidden in a trap-door safe. There is," Carrington fished a slip of paper from his trouser pocket, "by his accounting, ten thousand, one hundred and twenty-five dollars, exactly, in this strongbox. And with it a note that this money belongs to you."

That was enough for Captain Scott. He raised his hand to strike the colonel. Slocum, seeing the move, stepped in, taking the blow on the shoulder. Scott reached for his pistol. Before any of the troopers could recover from their surprise, Scott's pistol was cocked. He backed toward the hallway.

"If anyone moves, I'll shoot to kill," he said. "Emily, you pick up that strongbox and come with me."

"Emily, if you do it, you're as guilty as he is," said Slocum, his head all but cleared of the cobwebs. "Scott, you're a damned fool."

Raymond, his eyes raging with hatred, charged at that moment.

"Raymond, no!" shouted Slocum.

The ex-slave, oblivious to the danger, lowered his head as he raced across the room. Scott took deadly aim and fired.

Raymond's head exploded in a cloud of rosy spray. The black man's momentum hurled him forward. He crumpled and skidded lifelessly into the bookcase, dead before he came to a halt.

Slocum dove for his pistol on the settee.

The captain swung his pistol, fired blindly where Slocum had been.

Carrington, still poised, issued his command.

"Troopers, shoot that man if he does not drop his weapon at once. Captain Scott, I order you to—"

Slocum's fingers closed around the butt of his pistol. He jerked it from its holster, thumbed the hammer back.

A wraith-like figure appeared behind Scott.

Something silver flashed in the light.

Captain Scott opened his mouth wide. No sound came out. His eyes rolled back in their sockets. He twisted in agony.

Slocum froze.

A pair of scissors jutted from a place between the

captain's shoulder blades.

Behind him, Pearl wore a wan smile.

"He did it to me," she said softly. "He did terrible things to me."

Scott fell and writhed on the floor. He made croaking noises in his throat.

Slocum stood up and took Pearl into his arms.

He looked at Emily and Jennie. Emily began to sob. Jennie glared at him.

"You bastard," she hissed.

"Slocum," said Pearl. "Take care of me. Please."

"Yes," he said slowly, his eyes meeting Carrington's, "I'll take care of you."

She buried her face in Slocum's chest.

He put his arms around her and held her close as he watched Captain William F. Scott die on the floor.

He died in agony. He died very slowly.

And no one in the room made a move to help him.